SPECIAL MESSAGE TO READERS

THE ULVERSCROFT FOUNDATION
(registered UK charity number 264873)

was established in 1972 to provide funds for research, diagnosis and treatment of eye diseases. Examples of major projects funded by the Ulverscroft Foundation are:-

- The Children's Eye Unit at Moorfields Eye Hospital, London
- The Ulverscroft Children's Eye Unit at Great Ormond Street Hospital for Sick Children
- Funding research into eye diseases and treatment at the Department of Ophthalmology, University of Leicester
- The Ulverscroft Vision Research Group, Institute of Child Health
- Twin operating theatres at the Western Ophthalmic Hospital, London
- The Chair of Ophthalmology at the Royal Australian College of Ophthalmologists

You can help further the work of the Foundation by making a donation or leaving a legacy. Every contribution is gratefully received. If you would like to help support the Foundation or require further information, please contact:

THE ULVERSCROFT FOUNDATION
The Green, Bradgate Road, Anstey
Leicester LE7 7FU, England
Tel: (0116) 236 4325

website: www.foundation.ulverscroft.com

ENCHANTED NURSE

English nurse Karyn Gregory believes her new post on the Greek island of Sporveza will be a dream come true. But it's not all smooth sailing as she meets her challenging charge, Nerissa, a young woman haunted by the accident that caused the deaths of her parents. Unable to walk, she blames herself for the tragedy, hiding away in the gloomy attic of the cliffside house. And how is Nerissa's handsome brother, Paul, involved with the mysterious darker side of the island — one that is stained with blood?

PHYLLIS MALLET

ENCHANTED NURSE

Complete and Unabridged

LINFORD
Leicester

First published in Great Britain in 1969

First Linford Edition
published 2019

A catalogue record for this book is available
from the British Library.

ISBN 978–1–4448–4259–3

Published by
F. A. Thorpe (Publishing)
Anstey, Leicestershire

Set by Words & Graphics Ltd.
Anstey, Leicestershire
Printed and bound in Great Britain by
T. J. International Ltd., Padstow, Cornwall

This book is printed on acid-free paper

1

Karyn Gregory stood on the deck of the little islands steamer and stared at the blue Ionian Sea with wide eyes that held much of the same pale colour. This was all too good to be true, she told herself happily. After the winter months of England this warmth and brightness filled her with enchantment, and the feeling of a dream that was coming true still gripped her as it had done from the moment she accepted the post of nurse to a paralysed girl.

The island rising out of the brilliant sea before the ship was called Sporveza. It was Greek, lying north of Corfu and within sight of the mountains of Albania to the east. Karyn had studied the island in more than one atlas since accepting the post she was about to fill, and it seemed to her that at last one of her fondest dreams was coming true.

1

She had always been in love with this part of the world, ever since her father had brought her here as a child to see the country of her mother. She had the blonde, pale looks of her father's family, but there was much in her nature to show her mother's side. Although she hardly remembered her mother she had seen photographs of her, and knew that the Greek part of her ancestry had a large influence upon her outlook. Karyn could not understand some of the impulese that leaped to life inside her, but since starting out on this trip to take up her nursing post, she realized that Fate had taken a hand in her life and was even now conducting her forward into another phase that promised to be filled with beauty and joy.

She gripped the rail of the little ship and stared with narrowed eyes at the island. Was she feeling much the same emotions that had gripped the Romans and the Venetians when first they came to this part of the world to dominate and influence? Her long blonde hair blew in the sea wind like a fair pennant. The bright blue sea and sky matched her eyes, filling them with an extra lustre that seemed to glitter in the pale, liquid depths. She saw a dolphin in the water, circling, leaping and speeding forward, and she remembered her father, now dead, with a tiny pang of grief. He had introduced her to all of this, and his tales of her mother, when he had first met her in a Greece dominated by perhaps the most ruthless of all invaders, the Nazis, had awakened in Karyn a longing that never died. She knew that the reason she had accepted the post of nurse to Nerissa Stephan was the fact that she would be living on Greek soil.

As she watched the island growing larger, Karyn knew enchantment. It was too difficult and obscure for her to define it for herself, but she knew that the Greek part of her blood was fired by all this that her mother had known in momentous times. It had been on a similar island that her father, as a young

British army officer, had met the lovely Greek girl who sheltered him after the Germans had pushed the British out.

Entering the little harbour filled Karyn with happiness. She stared with interest at the colourful fishing boats tied up at the cobbled quay, her blue eyes wide with admiration at sight of the houses built in tiers among the wooded hills overlooking the bay. As the ship tied up she heard one of the crew members singing lustily in a beautiful bass voice, and the words-seemed to haunt her mind, the melody filling her with tremulous emotion.

She stared across the bay towards the western arm of high wooded land that sheltered the harbour and town from the storms that sometimes blew with intense ferocity. She had been told that the Stephan house stood on the clifftop overlooking the deep waters of the sea, a sentinel-like edifice that had stood for generations guarding the land against the unknown that had always lain close to Greece. She saw a tiny building perched on the extremity of the head-land, and felt a thrill of strange emotion as she stared at the black silhouette of turrets and was reminded of some ghostly castle that was inhabited by the souls of those long-dead builders who had toiled for posterity.

The stone jetty was alive with locals whose main interest was to see the faces of the newcomers from the ship, and as she followed a crew member ashore Karyn felt as if she were coming home instead of setting foot upon a strange island. Her luggage was carried to the quayside, and several dark faced men came forward to offer the services of their waiting vehicles. The crew member accepted the voluble offer of the fore-most and was helped to put Karen's luggage into the vehicle. Then the man, with flashing white teeth glinting in the bright Greek sunshine, took his leave and the taxi driver ushered Karyn into the cab. She spoke Greek fairly well, and gave the man the address of the Stephan house. She saw a spark of interest come into his dark eyes, and then he got behind the wheel and started the vehicle. The road was fairly good, and Karyn was thrilled by the scenery as the car started around the coastline.

She stared down into tiny, scalloped coves when the road passed close to the edge of the cliffs, and saw yellow sand stretched smooth and firm between the cliffs and the sea. Heavy boulders on the beach showed where the water worked its insidious way upon them, but out in deeper water jagged rocks showed blackly in the blue brilliance. An abundance of short pines grew almost to the water's edge in some places, and long strands of sea weed lay like sleeping snakes on the pale sand.

The large house on the lonely crag looked insecure as she approached, and Karyn couldn't help thinking that it seemed so close to the edge of the cliffs it was a wonder it didn't go sliding down to the sharp rocks waiting below. She caught her breath sharply as she stared down into the dizzy depths when the car swept around a sharp bend. The scene was heady, like sweet wine, and the brilliance of the sun hurt her unaccustomed eyes. She saw the driver staring at her in the rear view mirror, an indulgent smile upon his dark face, and he grinned as she returned his smile. They conversed in Greek, and Karyn told him a little of her background, to impress upon him that she was half Greek and could feel the magic of this wonderful little island, not as a tourist or ordinary visitor but as a daughter returning to the land of her birth.

When the car pulled into the driveway and stopped by a wide flight of yellow stone steps, Karyn got her first close look at the house. It was large, almost overwhelming, and the walls were golden, as if they had soaked up the sunshine and stored it through all the years of its being. It was cleanly built, with sharp lines and an atmosphere of the temple about it. The driver took her luggage and led the way up to a wide *piazza*. Here there was a sheer drop to the sea on the other side of the stone parapet, and Karyn gasped with pleasure as she stared out across the placid water. She glanced around at the many massive stone pots that were over-flowing with beautiful trailing plants, and she caught the sweet scent of flowers growing in a terraced garden that was beyond the *piazza*. Stone steps on the far side of the *piazza* led into the garden, and from there a path showed the way down to the beach far below, passing under an arbour of wild-grape.

Karyn took it all in with one encompassing glance, seeing the Oleanders hanging their rose-bells in the hot sunshine, the green and golden shades of the Cypresses and the clumps of fragrant morning glory. Small birds with wonderfully coloured wings were flitting among the green pepper trees. This was like Heaven, she told herself as the taxi driver set down her luggage on the threshold of the *salotto*. They entered the large room and she was fascinated by the heavy furniture.

A woman appeared through an inner doorway, medium, peasant-looking, with heavy features and very dark eyes. When she smiled her teeth glinted cleanly, and the taxi driver instantly took his leave.

'We have been expecting you, Miss Gregory,' the woman said in good English. 'I am Miranda Orestes, the housekeeper here. I have prepared a room for you. I expect you are tired after your trip from England.' Her stare was curious and unabashed in the way of the Greeks, but there was friendliness in her eyes, and Karyn smiled in return.

'I'm so happy to be here. And how is the patient?'

'Not at all well. No doubt Mr Paul will tell you all about her before you meet her, but I feel I should warn you that your task here is a very difficult one, and I wish you success for your own sake as well as for Nerissa's. Let me take your smaller cases and my husband will bring up the others when he comes in from the garden.'

'Tell me about Nerissa Stephan,'

Karyn said as she followed the woman to the stairs that led to the upper floors. As she expected, there were many passages and unexpected doors in this old building, and everywhere the furniture was dark and carved, old fashioned and so fitting in with the atmosphere of the house. When they came to the room where she was to sleep, Karyn found that it was at the front of the house with a vast view of the sea far below. It was a frightening aspect, but she knew she would come to love it in time. The house was so close to the edge of the cliff that it seemed about to leap into the void at its foundations, and when Karyn leaned out of the window at the housekeeper's bidding she found nothing but the *piazza* between her and the depths to the surface of the sea.

'You will get used to it,' Miranda Orestes said with a smile. She was about forty, already showing signs of age, although Karyn could see that she had been beautiful in her youth. 'I won't tell you about Nerissa, except to say that she is on the verge of total breakdown. I don't know if you've heard anything at all about the tragedy that took her parents and ruined her life, but it is simply told. The facts are cold and hard, and give you nothing of the heartbreak that Nerissa has suffered. Paul was not on the boat at the time, but the death of his parents has affected him inside. It was a miracle that Nerissa was not drowned in the same storm that took her parents, but the miracle didn't save her from paralysis that has existed even though her broken leg is now healed and as good as before. She will never get well. She lives in the top room, just above here, and she doesn't leave it from one week to another. She spends her days staring out at the sea which claimed her mother and father, and no medicine in the world will restore her. I am beginning to think that it would be a blessing if she could die. I have been like a mother to her from the day she

11

was born. She took the place in my heart of the children I could never have, and now she is like a broken sail. There is no hope in her.'

'I have been given the details of the boating tragedy,' Karyn said. 'It must have been dreadful for Nerissa. She's barely twenty-two now, is she?'

'That's right. In three months she will be twenty-two.'

'And the tragedy occurred eighteen months ago?'

'That is correct.' Miranda Orestes turned to the door, shaking her dark head. 'I don't think there is anything you can do to help Nerissa. She wants nothing and will have nothing beyond the bare necessities to sustain her life. Doctor Christos comes to see her once each week, but there is nothing he can do. No doubt he will tell you that Nerissa can only help herself.'

'It's terrible,' Karyn said slowly. 'But if I can make her life a little more bearable then it will be worth it. Poor girl! What she must have suffered.'

'We all have to suffer a little,' came the gentle reminder, and Karyn nodded soberly. 'Paul will return here later this afternoon. He wanted to meet you at the quayside, but he is running the shipping business now that his father is dead, and he finds it a difficult occupation. He wasn't intended for business. He is not happy unless he has a paint brush in his hand.'

'I heard that he is an artist with considerable talent,' Karyn said.

'Not any more. He doesn't work at his art, and hasn't done so since the tragedy. I hope I'm not colouring the atmosphere here against your attitude. This old house takes some getting used to. I hope you will settle down and can help Nerissa.'

'That's all I hope to do,' Karyn replied.

'Good. You will find me somewhere around no matter the time of day or night. If you should need anything then you have only to call or ring. My husband will also be ready to help you.'

13

'Thank you, Miranda. May I call you Miranda?'

'Please do. And you are Karyn. That is a Greek name, is it not?'

'Yes. My mother was Greek.' Karyn smiled, and saw an answering light in the housekeeper's eyes.

'Then you will understand what is happening here,' Miranda said slowly. 'Perhaps you will be able to do something for our little Nerissa. She badly needs help, if only someone could find the right method.'

'I shall do my best,' Karen promised soulfully, and she meant it.

Miranda departed silently, and Karyn began to unpack her cases. She went to the window several times to look down at the glittering sea, and each time she leaned from the window she experienced the most thrilling sensation in her stomach. There was a drop of at least two hundred feet to the surface of the sea, but as Miranda had said, she would get used to it. She relaxed for a moment, casting her mind back to

14

England. There was nothing there to hold her. With her father's death she had been left alone. She had subconsciously hoped to get away from all that she knew, and she felt that Fate had been responsible for this post being offered to her. Now she was here and the past was a closed door at her back. The future was laid before her, strange and mysterious, and there was a gentle stirring in her mind as she hoped that she would find the right method of approach to Nerissa Stephan. She had been warned that her charge was most difficult, and the fact that she had been engaged upon a temporary basis proved it.

There was a tap at the door, and when Karyn opened it she found a tall, powerful man standing there, holding the rest of her luggage. He introduced himself as Michael Orestes, the gardener and manservant, and carried her cases into the room.

'I hope you will like it here, Miss Gregory,' he said in pleasant tones. His eyes were deep and dark, like his wife's, and they showed the same amount of friendliness. 'It will be a great pity if nothing can be done to help Nerissa. We are all praying for a miracle. Perhaps you will be able to procure one.' He smiled, his teeth gleaming against the darkness of his skin. 'If I may say so, you don't look at all like any of the other nurses who have tried to handle Nerissa. You seem to be much too young, and you're very lovely.'

'Thank you. I take that as a compliment,' Karyn said with a laugh. 'Perhaps I shall be able to procure a miracle. At any rate I will do my best.'

'Master Paul has just returned from Lanios,' he said. 'If you are ready to meet him now I will take you along to his study.'

'I am ready,' Karyn said, and left the room with him. 'This is a wonderful old house, isn't it? I was dizzy looking from the window. Is the house perfectly safe up here?'

'It hasn't once fallen into the sea in

its eighty years,' came the suave reply, and Karen laughed lightly, nodding her head in agreement with his attitude towards the fact that what might happen in the future was not to be considered too deeply. 'The house has been in the Stephan family from its origin. Paul's grandfather had it built as a young man, and brought Paul's grandmother here from the mainland. You have Greek blood in you, so Miranda tells me. You must share our love of the past and the pleasure we derive from romancing about it.'

'I do!' Karyn said eagerly. 'I've never felt so happy in all my life as when I arrived in Greece. The trip from the mainland was wonderful, and I couldn't help feeling that I had experienced it all before.'

'Your blood probably did,' he enthused. 'I am certain that you will do what others have tried but failed to accomplish. If only Nerissa will take to you! That will be half the battle. I don't know what will happen to her if she doesn't. Perhaps it will mean the end of her, and such a pity, because she is a beautiful girl and had so much to look forward to before the tragedy.'

They reached the ground floor, and he paused at a heavy door and rapped sharply upon the centre panel. When a loud voice bade them enter he opened the door with a smile and stepped aside, indicating that Karyn should enter. When she did he closed the door at her back, remaining outside.

Karyn looked around the room with mounting interest, finding it large and tastefully furnished. There were tall bookshelves upon three walls, reaching from floor to high ceiling, and each shelf was crammed with books of all sizes. The fourth wall contained a large modern window that gave a wonderful view of the sea, and at the desk set before the window sat a youngish man who was regarding her intently. There was a faint smile on his lips as he watched her appraisal of the room, and then he got to his feet and came towards her, one hand stretched, his dark eyes showing admiration and relief.

'Nurse Gregory,' he said as Karyn took his hand. 'I'm so glad that you've arrived safely. I'm Paul Stephan. I hope you like your room.'

'It's wonderful,' she replied.

'And you think you'll like it here?' There was a tension in him that he tried to conceal, but it showed to Karyn's keen gaze.

'I don't have to think about that,' she told him frankly. 'My mother was Greek. I have an affinity for these islands.'

'Good! That at least is a major obstacle out of the way. I've had several English nurses for my sister, and none of them has really settled down to the climate or the scenery. Apart from that my sister is most difficult. Won't you sit down? I think I'd better paint you a clear picture before you meet Nerissa.'

He pulled forward a high backed chair for Karyn and she sat down, her eyes upon his dark, handsome face. His black hair was tightly curled, showing thick at his temples, and she told herself that he was certainly the most attractive man she had ever met.

'Your engagement was made on a temporary basis not because you may prove to be unsuitable but because my sister may become too much for you. It is a chance for you to change your mind about nursing her if after a few weeks you do find her intolerable. No doubt the agency explained to you about my sister, but she is much worse than any report could show.'

'I'm sure your sister's condition and attitude won't affect me in that way,' Karyn felt constrained to say. I'm a nurse and I do my work to the best of my ability. I can understand what you sister must be suffering, and I shall endeavour to do all I can to help her. You won't find me crying off just because I have a difficult patient on my hands.'

'Good.' He smiled, and for a moment the harsh lines etching his face disappeared and he looked several years younger. Karyn had already estimated his age at about thirty-five, but now she changed her mind. He couldn't be that old! Perhaps worry and care had added to his appearance. 'So you think you can handle Nerissa. Well I certainly hope you're right. Shall we go up and meet her now?'

'Yes please.' Karyn nodded emphatically. She had heard a lot about this crippled girl, and now that she had arrived she couldn't wait any longer to accept the challenge.

He got to his feet, and for a moment he towered above Karyn, pausing at the side of the desk to look down into her blue eyes. She felt dwarfed as she gazed up into his tanned face, and a pulse started pounding in her temple. As she followed him to the door she found herself wondering about him. There was an air of remoteness about him that jarred with the picture she had made in her mind from her first snap judgement. But tragedy had taken its toll of

21

him, and she realized that he must be carrying a tremendous burden. Sympathy for him came to life inside her, and strengthened her determination to do what she could for this unfortunate, crippled girl who had lost the desire to live.

'This is a beautiful old house,' she observed as they ascended the wide stairs. 'It has such a wonderful atmosphere.'

'You've noticed that?' He glanced at her, and there was more relief in his face. 'The other nurses found it too overwhelming. One said that it is haunted, and wouldn't stay another minute under its roof than was necessary. But you don't look the type to be afraid of ghosts.'

'It's a matter of attitudes,' Karyn retorted with a smile. 'I'm not afraid of that sort of thing.'

They reached the top floor, and there was another flight of stairs, much narrower and less ornate than the lower ones, leading up to the attics. As they ascended these stairs there was a sudden outburst of high pitched shouting, and a crash as something heavy was dropped. The next instant Miranda, the housekeeper, appeared above them and came hurrying down the stairs in high dudgeon, muttering swiftly in Greek. She halted instantly when she saw Karyn and Paul Stephan, and then broke out into a flow of angry chatter.

'All right, Miranda,' Paul said soothingly. 'We're going up to see Nerissa. Leave it to us. I somehow think Nurse Gregory will have Nerissa's measure. At least we must hope so, because this is Nerissa's last chance. If she doesn't settle down and start showing normal progress then I shall have her sent to a hospital on the mainland.'

The threat stopped the housekeeper's tirade, and she quickly began to plead for leniency, her dark eyes glancing at Karyn, who nodded sympathetically.

'Don't worry, Miranda,' she said gently. 'I think I'll be able to find the way through to Nerissa.'

'I have been praying that someone with the necessary understanding would

23

come here,' the woman replied devoutly. 'Perhaps you can help that poor girl.' She shook her head and went on down the stairs, and Paul stared after her for a moment before sighing heavily and continuing up the stairs.

When they reached a narrow landing Karyn heard the sound of unrestrained sobbing. She reached out a hand and touched Paul Stephan's arm as he moved to open a door. He glanced at her, his expression closed, controlled, but there was much in his eyes to show Karyn that he felt deeply for his crippled sister.

'Let me go in alone and introduce myself,' she said softly.

He stared at her for a moment, considering it, and then he nodded. He stepped aside, and Karyn took a deep breath as she entered the room. She closed the door at her back and leaned against it, staring around quickly, narrowing her eyes against the gloom, because heavy curtains were drawn across the windows. She saw that the furniture up here was in the same fashion as the rest of the house, but this room seemed to have a brooding air about it, as if this poor girl's imprisoned spirit was filling it with the hopelessness which it felt.

The girl lying in the bed was indistinct to Karyn's eyes. But her sobbing was real enough, and a pang struck through Karyn as she went forward. There was a heavy tray lying upturned on the floor, and the patient's tea was strewn all over the thick carpet. The room smelled as if the windows had been shut tightly for weeks, and it was oppressive, not at all the ideal atmosphere for a sick room.

'Is there anything I can do for you?' Karyn said firmly, and the girl in the bed jerked in surprise and lifted her dark head. Her sobbing stopped instantly, and Karyn was subjected to a close scrutiny. She remained silent and still, waiting for the girl to speak.

'What are you doing in here without my permission?' The words, when they came, were passionate and heartrending. There was raw emotion in the tones, the harshness of a lonely, over-burdened spirit that was crying out for aid.

'Your brother was bringing me up to meet you,' Karyn said slowly. 'I thought you wouldn't want him to see you in this state so I came in alone. I'm Karyn Gregory, your new nurse.'

'I don't need a nurse, so don't bother to unpack. Paul will see that you return to where ever you came from. You're English, aren't you? You speak very well.'

'My mother was Greek,' Karyn said, moving to the side of the rumpled bed automatically straightening the covers.

'Don't do that! Get out of here and leave me alone with my misery. You have no right in here.'

'I only want to help you. I think you've been left too much alone. Haven't you been miserable long enough?'

'Haven't they told you about my parents? How they were killed and I survived? Don't think I'm just lying here feeling sorry for myself because I'm not. I'm crippled. I can't walk. My legs are paralysed. It was God's way of punishing me because I lived when my parents died.'

'That's not true!' Karyn spoke gently but firmly, aware of the hysteria in the girl.

'What do you know about it?'

'My parents are dead. My mother was killed in a car accident so long ago that I can hardly remember her. My father died not so long ago. I do know what you must be feeling. That's why I'm here, and I think I can help you, Nerissa.'

'I don't need help. I'm past all aid,' the girl said in quivering tones. 'Just leave me alone. That's all I ask. I want to be left alone.'

'I'll tidy up in here,' Karyn said, turning to lift the tray. 'If this is a sick room then it should be treated as such. Didn't you want this food on the tray? Is there something else you would prefer? I'm sure we can arrange anything.'

'All I want is to be left alone.' There was anguish in the shrill tones, and

Karyn nodded slowly, taking the tray as she went to the door.

'I'll go now, but I shall come to you later,' she promised, and departed slowly, sighing as she closed the door at her back.

2

Paul Stephan turned anxiously as Karyn emerged from the room. His worried face showed so much strain that Karyn felt pity well up in her heart. He stared at her, wondering how she had managed, and Karyn smiled as she carried the tray down the stairs.

'She's upset at the moment,' she said slowly. 'I'll go back to her in a few minutes.'

'What do you think of her?' he demanded. 'Do you think you will be able to do anything with her?'

'It will take time, whatever happens,' Karyn replied. 'She has been left too long in her misery.'

'There was nothing I could do about that,' he confessed. 'I did everything she asked, put her up there in the top of the house, fetched everything she said she wanted, and left her alone when she demanded solitude. So I've done wrong in those things. But you know more about this business than I, so I look to you to set me straight.'

'Isn't there a more pleasant room in the house?' Karyn demanded. 'Doesn't she ever leave the house? Won't she come out into the garden?'

'She won't leave that room. Doctor Christos has been berating me for not following his advice by sending Nerissa into a hospital on the mainland. But I feel the girl has suffered too much already, and leaving here, where all her ties are so strong, might have the opposite effect. Doctor Christos has told me this. It is a gamble that I have not been prepared to accept. But if you fail to make progress with Nerissa then I shall have to act as the doctor suggests. I think it will be the end of my sister, but this state of affairs cannot be permitted to continue.'

Miranda was waiting at the bottom of the stairs, and she took the tray from Karyn with a murmur of thanks.

'At least she didn't throw things at you,' the housekeeper said. 'That's all I get. I don't know if you'll manage to do what we want, Karyn, but you have my sympathies.'

The woman hurried away, and Karyn looked up into Paul's face. The worry she saw there stiffened her determination, and she squared her shoulders as she thought over her first impressions of the girl. Her sympathies were aroused and she knew she could not turn down this challenge. Perhaps he saw something of her thoughts in her expression, for he spoke quickly, anxiously.

'Do you think she will be too much for you?' he demanded.

'Certainly not! We'll need patience, but I think I can win her around. Once I have her confidence we can make a start on the miracle that Miranda prays for.'

He smiled, nodding his head. 'If you can perform that miracle for my sister then everything I have is yours for the asking. Personally I don't think this is possible, but I live in hope, and if there's anything you want or need then don't hesitate to mention it. I'll do anything you ask if it will be in Nerissa's interests. You have a free hand, Nurse Gregory.'

'Thank you. Then if you'll excuse me I'll go back up to Nerissa and see what I can do.' Karyn smiled at him and turned to ascend the stairs. She was aware that he stared keenly after her, and she felt a flicker of hope that he would not be too disappointed in her efforts to help his sister.

Opening the door of the sick room, Karyn entered and paused on the threshold. She could see Nerissa's still form on the bed, and closed the door softly. The girl gave no indication of having seen her, and the brooding silence in the room was over-powering. Karyn approached the bed and stood at its foot, staring at the girl.

'I'd like to introduce myself,' she said gently. 'I'm Karyn Gregory. You're

Nerissa Stephan.' She paused, but there was no reply. 'Shall I open the curtains to let some light into the room? This can't do your eyes any good.'

'No!' The single word cracked from the girl's lips. 'I like this gloom. It matches my thoughts and my mood. If you want to help me then leave me alone. Go away.'

Karyn walked to the window and pulled open the curtains, permitting a flood of golden sunlight to fill the room. The girl uttered a cry of anger and disappeared under the bed clothes. Karyn looked around the room, and the first thing she saw was a wheelchair in a corner. She nodded slowly, her lips pursed, and started tidying the room, which was littered with things Merissa had found in her reach and had thrown in temper. She kept silent, and by the time the room was neat and clean several minutes had passed. She kept her eyes averted from the bed, although she was curious to see this girl who had suffered so greatly.

When she started tidying the bed covers again Nerissa came up for air, and stared at Karyn, a mixture of curiosity and bad temper in her expression. Karyn found herself looking at a very beautiful face, although it was pale and wan, with dark circles beneath the large brown eyes.

'Hello,' she said cheerfully. 'What beautiful hair you've got. It's in need of brushing, but it's beautiful. Do you fix it yourself?'

The girl made no reply, and there was a sullen pout to her curved lips. Karyn went to the dressing table and picked up a brush. She returned to the bed expecting a fight, but the girl said nothing as she sat down and began to brush the extremely long black hair.

'I've come all the way from England to take care of you,' Karyn said. 'I expect you've been lonely up here with nothing to do but look down at the sea.'

'I like it up here, and I prefer my own company,' the girl retorted. 'I don't care about my hair or the way I look. Why don't you leave me alone?'

'Because I have a job to do,' Karyn retorted firmly. 'I'll make a bargain with you, Nerissa, if you like.'

'About what?' There was a rebellious note in the musical voice, but it was edged with curiosity.

'I have to stay here and take care of you, but I promise I won't bother you too much if you help me to help you.'

'So that's to be your method of getting around me, is it?' Nerissa demanded, smiling thinly. 'You think to win my confidence and my friendship, then you hope to accomplish what the others failed to do.'

'I expect they were only wanting to help you, Nerissa, just as I do. Don't you want to be helped?'

'It is useless. I am not to be helped. This is my punishment. Can't you understand that? My brother does not understand. Miranda doesn't care. But this is my cross that I have to bear and I will keep it. I don't want your help or your friendship. Go away and leave me alone.'

Karyn continued brushing the girl's hair, and Nerissa subsided again. The silence in the room was heavy, but the sunlight made it appear more pleasant.

'At what time of the day do you have your bath?' Karyn asked suddenly.

'I don't. There's no bathroom up here and Miranda can't get me down the stairs to the next floor. I have a bed bath, and make do with that, although Miranda grumbles all the time.'

'But you haven't always had this room, have you?' Karyn demanded. 'Surely you have one of those nice bedrooms below here!'

'I did, but I moved up here after the accident. Now stop asking questions. I don't want my hair brushed any more.' Nerissa snatched at the brush and threw it across the room. It thudded against the wall just as the door opened, and Paul Stephan entered and bent to retrieve it. He came across to the bed and handed it to Karyn, who smiled and resumed brushing Nerissa's hair.

'Don't you think it would be more

fitting if you showed some sign of hospitality to Nurse Gregory?' Paul demanded stiffly. 'These bad manners of yours are too bad, Nerissa. You forget yourself.'

'It's all right,' Karyn said gently. 'She is a sick girl and we must make allowances for her.'

'Very well.' Paul shrugged and stood at the foot of the bed, staring down at his sister. She stared back at him with aggression in her face, and Karyn felt that she could accept the fact that Paul himself was partly to blame for the girl's manner.

'Perhaps you've had enough of me for one day,' she said to the girl, getting to her feet and returning the hair brush to its place on the dressing table. 'But I should like to get you into a bath.' She looked at Paul. 'Is there any way of getting Nerissa into the bathroom on the floor below?'

'The easiest way would be for her to return to her old bedroom down there,' he replied. 'But as far as she's concerned that is out of the question. She likes to make her own life difficult as well as complicating mine. This is her punishment, as no doubt she has already told you. But what she didn't say was that she's punishing everyone else as well. I keep hoping that this childishness will pass, but now the time has come for me to face up to facts. Nerissa, you've had several nurses in the past few months, and none of them has been suitable, according to you. But you must make do with Nurse Gregory, because if she decides that you are too difficult to handle then you will go to the hospital on the mainland that Doctor Christos is always talking about.'

'I won't leave this house,' the girl said sullenly.

'You will if I decide that it will be for your own good, Nerissa,' he retorted firmly. 'So just bear that in mind. If you don't change your ways then your days in this house are numbered. It will be a very long time before you ever get back.'

Karyn watched the girl's face, and saw the glint of tears in the dark eyes. Paul Stephan stared at his sister for several moments, their eyes showing the clash of wills, and then he turned away and departed. As the door closed at his back Nerissa burst into tears and averted her face. Karyn let the girl cry, hoping that it would relieve her pent up feelings, and by degrees Nerissa regained her composure.

'They are all against me,' she whispered slowly. 'I have done a great wrong, and to add to my suffering I must see my own brother's unhappiness.'

'What is this great wrong that you keep talking about?' Karyn demanded.

'They have told you about the tragedy?' the girl countered.

'Yes. But that wasn't your fault, surely!'

'It was. I suggested the trip. I was handling the boat at the time of the accident. My parents were drowned but I was flung unconscious upon the beach down there. That's why I have this room. I can see the exact spot where the boat hit the rocks, and I can suffer all the torments that are due to me. It cannot be any other way, so you are wasting your time here with me.'

'But are you forgetting your brother's words?' Karyn demanded. 'Don't you believe him when he says you are to go into a hospital if I can't help you?'

'I believe him, and if I have to leave here then it will only be part of my punishment.' Nerissa turned her face to the window, and Karyn could see tears glittering in the girl's eyes. 'I don't care what happens to me, she said softly, her tiny white teeth biting into her bottom lip.

'Have you no friends?' Karyn questioned. 'Doesn't anyone visit you here?'

'I had friends before the accident, but they all stay away now.' Nerissa laughed, a malicious, unpleasant sound. 'I scared them all away with my manner. They think I am crazy now and won't come near me.'

'Was there any special friend?'

The girl did not reply at once, and Karyn almost regretted the question when she saw the distress coming into Nerissa's face. But she said nothing, hoping that the girl would begin to talk of her own free will.

'There was, once,' came the hesitant reply. 'But I expect he has found another girl by this time.'

'What is his name?'

'Nikos Ellas. Please don't ask me questions. I have too much pain in trying to forget the past without having it all dragged up against my will.'

'I'm sorry.' Karyn reached out and took hold of the girl's hand, and for a moment she could feel the rejection that flooded through Nerissa. Then a sob tore loose in the girl's throat and she clung to Karyn's hand as she broke down and cried bitterly.

Karyn stroked the long silky hair, saying nothing, hoping that this was a good sign. She knew she has to handle this situation with the utmost delicacy. It would be like feeling her way through a darkened, unfamiliar room, and the slightest mistake or even a wrong word would place her in an irretrievable position. There was a strong challenge in this situation, but there was more at stake than just her job. This girl's whole future lay in the balance, and if she could not be pulled back out of the shadows then she would be utterly lost for the rest of her life.

By degrees the sobbing abated, and finally the girl lifted her face and stared at Karyn.

'I'm so miserable,' she said huskily. 'I wish I were dead.'

'I know how you must be feeling,' Karyn said softly, and filled with impulse, she pulled the girl's head gently towards her shoulder. 'I'll do what I can to help you, Nerissa, she went on. 'But you must help yourself, too. There are two ways in which to live, and you're choosing the hardest. I don't blame you for feeling the way you do, but I understand, and if you'll let me then I'll do what I can to help.'

'You're not like the other nurses I've had,' the girl said, her voice muffled with her face pressed against Karyn's shoulder. 'They treated me as if I were mental.'

'Well I'll give you a chance to show me what you can do,' Karyn said firmly. 'You have to show your brother that you're not helpless. I think you can look forward to changes now that I'm here. It may be difficult, but I think we can put you back on the road to recovery.'

'I'll never be the same as before the accident,' the girl said quickly.

'That's true, but you won't have the nightmare in your mind that's been haunting you ever since it happened.'

'You know about that?' Nerissa lifted her face and stared into Karyn's blue eyes. 'You must be telling the truth when you say you know how I feel if you can tell me what's in my mind. I didn't like the others. They didn't understand. But you're so different. I'm sorry for the way I acted when you came in. I'm sorry for a lot of things.'

She lowered her head and began to cry again, and Karyn held her gently, soothing her with a firm hand upon a slim shoulder. There was sympathy inside her, and hope. This breakdown could be the first great step for the girl, and Karyn knew in her heart that although it might be a tough fight, Nerissa would recover.

'Shall I get you some food now?' she asked when the girl had regained her composure.

'I don't think I want anything,' came the hesitant reply. Dark eyes in a tear streaked face peered up at Karyn. 'But perhaps I should try something. I do feel unbelievably weak.'

'Then I'll go down to the kitchen and see what I can get. Miranda will tell me your likes and dislikes. You lie back now and rest, and tomorrow we shall see about organising your days to give you pleasure. You must have been terribly bored and lonely up here at the top of the house.'

'I like it up here because I don't hear

the sound of the sea.' The girl shuddered, and Karyn warned herself not to try and push too hard to start with. She could overdo it, and then her attempts to assume power over the situation might have the opposite effect.

'I had a shock when I leaned out of my bedroom window,' Karyn said in conversational tones. 'I felt really dizzy looking down at the sea. You've got a beautiful view from up here.'

'I never look now. I'm terrified of the sea after what happened.'

'Never mind, we'll see what we can do to improve your outlook. It's only a matter of time and patience. We'll soon have you taking an interest in things.' Karyn got slowly to her feet. As she walked to the door she saw the girl watching her closely. 'Tell me some of the things you used to like doing,' she said.

A slow smile spread against Nerissa's face, and she shook her head regretfully. 'I'm afraid those days will never come back to me,' she said. 'Things will never be the same. So much happened, and death changed my life. There's no way to get around death. If my parents were still alive it would be different, but we can't set back the hands of the clock. Even God couldn't do that.'

'We have to learn to live with our grief,' Karyn said, and her voice quivered with sudden emotion.

'You told me your parents are dead.' There was a note of interest in the girl's tones, and Karyn nodded, more hopeful now.

'Yes. I had to make the very decisions that face you now. I really do know how you're feeling, and I wish I could give you the benefit of my experience. But I can't say to you, look, try and forget what's happened and concentrate upon rebuilding your life into a good future. Other people might say that, but it would prove they didn't understand. All I can say, in the light of what happened to me, is, do try and look forward. You will find it difficult, but at least take comfort from the knowledge that others

46

had to travel the same road. Think of other people and try to understand how they're feeling. As soon as you can forget about yourself you'll be taking the very first step. What about your brother? Have you considered how he must be feeling about your parents and about you? Don't you think it would help him if you began to mend and resume your former self?'

'Yes.' Nerissa spoke softly. Her dark eyes seemed luminous in the bright sunshine flooding the room. 'I can see what you mean. I'm beginning to feel different already, just listening to you. I do want to be helped. Promise that you will do as you say.'

'I promise,' Karyn said readily. 'Remember that I shall be here ready to run to your side.'

'Thank you.' Tears streamed down the girl's face again, and Karyn smiled, for this was a different kind of crying. She turned and tiptoed from the room and went down to the kitchen, leaving the crippled girl to make the first tentative steps along the road to recovery alone. There was no other way that Nerissa could do it. The first attempt had to be a lonely affair.

Down in the kitchen, where she found Miranda busily engaged in preparing the evening meal, Karyn explained what she had done, and saw astonishment flood the housekeeper's dark, passionate features.

'Truly you are the nurse we've been waiting for,' she said in awed tones. 'No-one has been able to do anything with Nerissa. But tread carefully, for the path is long and treacherous. There are days when I dare not even go to that room where she lies.'

'I'll be careful,' Karyn promised. 'But I hope to have her out of that attic and back in her own room before very long. Now prepare another tray for Nerissa, Miranda, and I'll see that she starts eating her meals.'

The housekeeper nodded enthusiastically. 'The miracle has started,' she said strongly. 'I have the feeling that the

48

saints have blessed you. Even Paul seems different now that you're here. You're almost one of us, Karyn. There's our kind of blood running through your veins. Perhaps you have come to this island to meet your destiny!'

3

Karyn thought over the housekeeper's words while she attended to Nerissa, and there was a smile on her lips as she watched her patient eating half heartedly the meal which she had brought up to her. Karyn didn't believe in Destiny as such. She had never been a fanciful girl. But she knew that something had happened to her the moment she reached Greek waters. Her heart had seemed to lighten, her habitual staid inner self had begun to mellow, and the process was still going on. She felt totally different inside, and knew it was because she had come to her mother's country to live. England was so far away, and remote in her mind. She had never made close friends with anyone there, and romance had never entered her life.

When she settled Nerissa down for the night she went below, and Miranda came to her, enquiring after the girl. She was relieved at Karyn's words, and declared again that a miracle was taking place.

'I am about to serve the evening meal,' the housekeeper said. 'Paul wants you to eat with him on the *piazza*. He always dines out there late in the evening. I am so glad you are here, for his sake, because he has always been a lonely one. But with you in the house he will begin to come out of his shell. You are going to perform a great service for the Stephan family, I am sure of it.'

'I'm only doing my job,' Karyn protested. 'Is the meal ready? Do I have time to freshen up?'

'Yes. When you come down again I will call Paul and serve the meal.'

Karyn went up to her room, and crossed to the window to peer out at the wonderful Greek night. The first stars were beginning to show in the darkening sky, and they were so large and bright she felt that she had only to reach out of the window to touch them. As she changed into a deep necked, flame coloured dress she caught sight of her reflection in the large dressing table mirror, and she paused and studied her glowing features. Her blue eyes were filled with dancing light. She was being uplifted by that undefinable emotion which had come to life in her such a short time before. Nursing was her whole life, she told herself, but it wasn't the thought of what she could do with Nerissa that was buoying her up. There was a deeper reason in her mind that was vague and unreal, almost dormant yet ready to burst into prominence at the first flash of encouragement.

She sighed as she checked her make up. Then she went down the wide stairs, looking forward to meeting Paul again. She felt that she could report progress even at this early moment, and there was a gladness inside her because she could feel so confident about her patient.

The *piazza* was aglow with soft,

shaded light, and a table was set with three places. Karyn paused on the threshold of the little courtyard and looked around with pleasant surprise. Wall lanterns gave the area a fairylike appearance, and there was a small illuminated fountain in one corner, the sound of the slowly running water creating a gentle background to the beautiful scene. The space between the cliff top and the sea was dark, an admirable backcloth to the setting, and above the impenetrable darkness the starry sky glittered with myriad points of crystal light. Far away on the distant horizon a thin crescent of pale yellow moon was beginning to make its glow seen.

Karyn caught her breath, filled with an enchantment that had never before been hers to experience. She heard a slight sound in the shadows by the parapet, and came back to earth quickly, narrowing her eyes as she peered around. Then Paul showed himself, stepping forward into the lanternlight, tall and graceful in a dark lounge suit.

53

'Miranda has been telling me about your progress with Nerissa,' he said, advancing to her side. 'I agree that it is nothing short of a miracle. I wish you had come to us a long time ago, Nurse Gregory.' His tones were formal, and Karyn stiffened herself as he took her hand.

'Thank you Mr Stephan,' she replied. 'It is early yet to form an opinion of Nerissa, but the signs are hopeful. She's been dreadfully lonely here, and perhaps the other nurses were rather older than I. There's not much difference between Nerissa's age and mine, and I think she's taken an instant liking to me. So far so good!'

'Please call me Paul,' he said. 'Mr Stephan sounds so formal. And your name is Karyn. May I call you Karyn?'

'Please do!' She smiled and he laughed, and in that instant the stiff formality between them dissolved. 'I had to catch my breath when I came through that doorway,' she went on. 'What a beautiful place this is!'

'I'm so glad you like it. I hope you won't mind that I want to mix business with pleasure, but I've asked Doctor Christos to dine with us this evening. No doubt you will want to talk to him about Nerissa.'

'Yes. I'm so glad he's coming. I can't wait to hear what he has to say!'

'A car drew up a moment ago, and it must be him. May I get you a cocktail? Miranda will be serving the meal very soon now. But tell me how you managed to get Nerissa to eat?' He crossed the *piazza* with long strides and returned a moment later with a drink for Karyn. She thanked him as she took it from his steady fingers, and her heartbeats seemed to falter as their hands gently touched.

'It's fortunate that my manner seems to go down well with Nerissa,' she replied. 'I have to win her confidence, that's all. It's as simple as that, but very difficult to do.'

'I'm sure you will encounter no difficulties at all,' he retorted. 'You're most beautiful, Karyn, and I'm not surprised that Nerissa has taken to you.'

'Thank you.' Karyn smiled and sipped her drink. She heard footsteps in the house, and half turned to get her first look at Doctor Christos. What this man had to tell her would guide her attitude in nursing the girl. Karyn was conscious of a rush of anticipation as Miranda appeared, leading the doctor. On such a beautiful night, she told herself, what she learned about Nerissa could only be favourable. The gods would be watching from the shadowed heavens, and they could not but feel pity for the beautiful young girl condemned to a long life of emptiness.

Doctor Christos was a stocky, dark-eyed man looking very dapper in his white evening jacket. He came quickly on to the *piazza*, his eyes upon Karyn, and she took his small hand when Paul introduced them.

'Nurse Gregory, I am so happy to meet you,' he said in English. 'Perhaps you will be able to accomplish what the others failed to do.'

'I hope so, Doctor,' she replied in low tones, taking an instant liking to him. 'I'm impatient to learn the background of the case.'

'After we have eaten, please,' Paul said with a short laugh. 'No talking shop until afterwards. Miranda will not bless us if her cooking is ruined. A drink, Doctor?'

'Some of your excellent brandy, Paul.'

Karyn allowed herself to be seated at the table by Paul, and as she set down her wine glass their eyes met. She was surprised by the soft expression on his dark, handsome face. Was he already relieved at his sister's apparent progress? Karyn smiled slowly, vowing to herself that she would spare no effort to help his sister. No matter how difficult Nerissa proved to be, Karyn would find the necessary patience to help the girl along.

The meal that was served to them seemed like the food of the gods to

Karyn, and she felt enchanted as she listened to the conversation of the two men. Doctor Christos was interested in her, and she had to answer many questions about her life in England and her training as a nurse. Paul would not be left out of it, and by the time Miranda came to clear away the dishes Karyn felt that her whole past life had been brought out and aired. She sat watching Paul's shadowed face, trying to impress his features upon her mind, and she was aware that his brown eyes rarely left her face.

'Now let us talk about Nerissa,' Doctor Christos said. 'I can only tell you, Nurse Gregory, that there is precious little any doctor can do for the girl. Her trouble is in the mind. She suffered broken legs in the accident, but they have healed normally. The fact that she cannot walk points to physical inability, but I assure you that Nerissa could get out of bed this very moment and walk anywhere on the island, if only she wanted to.'

'You've told me this many times, Doctor,' Paul said curtly. 'But if this is in the mind why can't Nerissa fight it?'

'Because she doesn't want to.' The doctor leaned back in his seat and regarded Karyn with narrowed eyes. 'Your task will be to get her interested again in life. She feels a great guilt about the death of her parents, and she believes that by lying as a cripple for the rest of her days she is suffering for her guilt.'

'What happened when the accident occurred?' Karyn asked slowly. 'It won't pain you to give me the details, will it?'

'No.' Paul shook his head. 'I've got used to the knowledge now. That's why I have so much sympathy for poor Nerissa. I know what she's suffering, and it's worse because I can't do anything to help her. This business of her mind being at fault for her inability to walk is like so much black magic in my ears. I would pay any sum asked to have her cured.'

'I know that, Paul,' the doctor said

slowly. 'But all your money can't help little Nerissa. She doesn't need medicine. I don't know what it is that will help her, but perhaps your English nurse will find the answer.'

'Perhaps I will,' Karyn said slowly. 'But Nerissa is the only one in a true position to help herself.'

'True.' Doctor Christos leaned forward in his seat. 'The trouble is she doesn't want to be helped. Subconsciously she wants to stay a cripple.' He glanced at Paul. 'Perhaps you had better tell Nurse Gregory what happened at the time of the accident.'

'I will.' Paul sighed as he set down his glass. He watched Karyn with his keen brown eyes. 'My parents had gone sailing with Nerissa,' he said slowly. 'I was away on business at the time. Perhaps this would have ended differently had I been here, but that is beyond my ability to tell. There had been a storm for two days, and the wind was still high. From what I've pieced together from Nerissa's ravings in the days following the accident I believe that she lost her temper when my father at first refused to put to sea because of the waves, and she called him a coward. That was enough for my father. No doubt he wished to teach Nerissa a lesson. But he shouldn't have taken Mother along with them, unless she refused to stay behind. They went out, and Father suffered a heart attack. He lay unconscious in the boat while Mother tended him and Nerissa brought the craft back. It was impossible for her to get into the harbour at Khalmia, and such was Nerissa's panic, instead of making for the other side of the island, she tried to beach the yacht in the bay outside this house. It was madness to attempt it, and before they reached the shore the yacht overturned and went down.'

He paused for a moment, his eyes fixed upon Karyn's face. His own features were impassive, but there was a tightness about his mouth that told Karyn much. The doctor lifted his wine glass to his lips and sipped at the brandy. He leaned back in his seat as Paul continued.

'Nerissa had both legs broken when she was dashed against the rocks, but she was thrown upon the beach by a huge wave. Not so my parents. They were found on the beach three days later, still locked together. My mother had thrown her arms around my father as the yacht overturned, and thus they died.'

'How terrible!' Karyn was momentarily at a loss for words as she imagined the dreadful scene of the yacht going down. No wonder Nerissa has prayed to die! Now she could understand why the girl's mind had acquired such a guilt complex. She was blaming herself because she had panicked in the storm and done the wrong thing. If she had tried to make the other side of the island her parents would not have drowned. But Karyn could see the choice that Nerissa had faced.

The girl had tried to get into shore in order to fetch medical aid for her father. She had known that time was precious and she had gambled upon a safe landfall.

'It was a calamitous experience for Nerissa,' Doctor Christos said. 'I wonder how any of us would have fared after such an incident? I have nothing but admiration for the girl. She did what she thought was the right thing, and it was not her fault that they failed to make it. But she should not have blamed herself like this. That is the situation you have to face, Nurse. If you can get through to Nerissa and rid her of that spot of guilt she will recover completely and become her normal self.'

'Poor girl!' Karyn shook her head wordlessly. 'And she's been living in a nightmare world ever since she recovered consciousness after the accident.'

'You have it exactly,' the doctor said. 'How do you feel about it now, Nurse? Do you think you can help her?'

'Certainly.' Karyn was positive. 'Even if she doesn't make a complete recovery, she can be helped a lot. I think I've made a favourable impression upon her, and once I have her confidence then anything could happen.'

'That's it,' Doctor Christos said firmly.

'Well I feel that you can do it if anyone can,' Paul said. 'I shall be behind you all the time, hoping and praying, and ready to do anything you think will help.'

'You can stop your worrying for a start, Paul,' the doctor said firmly. 'It won't help matters if you suddenly crack up. You're working too hard as it is. When are you going to take that holiday we've been talking about?'

'Shortly.' Paul smiled thinly. 'Now that Nurse Gregory is here perhaps I can afford to relax a bit. I don't mind telling you that Nerissa has been a great strain.'

'And so I should think! You lost your parents at the same time, don't forget,' Doctor Christos said with emphasis. 'You couldn't afford the luxury of Nerissa's complaint. You had to take over the business and keep the wheels turning. If you're not careful, Paul, Nurse Gregory may find you upon her very capable hands before she's through with Nerissa.'

Miranda appeared silently in the doorway leading into the house, and Doctor Christos stiffened as the housekeeper called his name.

'There is a call for you, Doctor. You're wanted at the Marfissa villa urgently.'

'This is a doctor's lot,' the short little man said, excusing himself and arising from the table. 'I have enjoyed your hospitality and regret that I cannot stay longer. But business is business. I hope you will settle down here, Nurse Gregory, and enjoy your stay while taking care of Nerissa.'

'Have no fear of that,' Paul said strongly. He was on his feet as the doctor departed. 'I shall see to it that the hours don't lag for our saviour. Come again, Doctor, and make it soon.'

With the doctor's departure a different atmosphere settled upon the *piazza*. Paul led Karyn to the parapet, where they stood looking down at the sea, dark and mysterious in the growing paleness of the rising moon. Several ships were to be seen only by their lights, and the warm night filled with many scents; the flowers in the gardens, the plants in the big stone pots, the climbing plants around the parapet — all added their exotic perfumes to the open sky, and they mingled in Karyn's nostrils to fill her with enchantment. She sighed heavily, her mind absorbing many new impressions.

'Do you think you will be happy here with us?' Paul demanded, and she looked into his shadowed features. He was tall and straight at her side, and she could sense the emotions burning in him. He was praying that she could help his sister, and Karyn felt the need to reassure him, to put an end to his worrying. She could imagine the kind of life he had been leading, his parents dead, his sister a cripple and edging into nervous and mental troubles. But there was still a long, hard road ahead of him, and Karyn found herself wishing that he could be spared the interminable waiting.

'I shall be very happy here,' she replied with just the faintest quiver in her voice. 'I only hope that I can justify my presence.'

'Isn't Nerissa showing improvement already?' he demanded.

'It's too early to say yet, but I'm keeping my fingers crossed.'

'Let us take a walk,' he suggested. 'The night is very young, and I am filled with a strange restlessness. I want to tell you all about my family, and learn about your life in England. Perhaps I may be able to give you some clue to the way Nerissa needs to be handled. If I have such an important pointer then I know it unconsciously, and it will only come out in the course of conversation. But you will not be on duty all the time. That I will not permit. You must learn to find your way around. We have a private beach here, and the pathway down to it passes through groves of cypresses and olives.

You have to see it in daylight to really appreciate it, but I'll show you the way now and you won't need a guide later.'

'It's a long way down to the beach,' Karyn ventured as he took her arm and led her across the *piazza* to the steps. They walked through the gardens to a path that zig-zagged down the face of the cliff, and the rising moon was gaining in brightness with each passing moment, showing Karyn the way below, making her breathless and dizzy with its revelation of deep space.

'You must be very careful along this path,' Paul said severely. 'Only a few weeks ago one of the local fishermen fell to his death from a similar path. There is a fishing village called Lanios on the other side of the bay here. I shall take you there sight-seeing when we have the time. I'm sure you'll find it most interesting. There are some ruins nearby which are supposed to be the remains of the temple of our island saint. Are you interested in that sort of thing?'

'Yes.' Karyn could not keep the eagerness out of her voice, and he laughed gently at her display of enthusiasm.

'I shan't have a difficult task to keep you amused,' he said. 'And that I must do or you will leave us here.'

'I'll never do that,' Karyn said quickly, suddenly too conscious of his arm upon her elbow. He was on the outside of the path, apparently unaware of the tremendous drop only feet away. She glanced at him, seeing that his face was well lit in the moonlight. He was smiling, his teeth glinting, and his face looked even more handsome in this soft atmosphere. 'Nursing is more than a job with me,' she went on hurriedly. 'I accept the challenge, and the only thing that will make me withdraw is Nerissa's attitude. If she finds that she doesn't like me then I would leave out of consideration for her.'

'Then I shall pray tonight that she will find you most favourable,' he told her gravely.

For a time there was a heavy silence between them, and Karyn found herself attracted to him. They were alone in the moonlight and he was a handsome Greek. Roman and Grecian history had always enchanted her at school, and here was a handsome male from that ancient line, unattached and with a great romantic potential. Karyn halted her thoughts there. It would never do to permit her feelings full rein in that direction. She was here for a very important purpose, and she couldn't allow herself to be sidetracked in the slightest. But she could not help wondering why he was unmarried. Surely the local girls had found him most eligible.

When they reached the beach the lulling sound of the small waves rolling against the sand was the perfect background to this dream-like night. Karyn glanced around, overwhelmed by the dark shadows, awed by the majesty of the natural scene. There was a smooth power, compulsive, encompassing, in the moonlight and the peacefulness, and she knew a stranger might live here for a hundred years and not know the wonders now filling her. It was natural for her to feel these things. Her instincts from her mother's ancestors were at play on this island. The Greek blood in her was rioting under the stresses of so many strange but inherently familiar things.

'I can sense that you're in love with all this,' Paul said suddenly, and the sound of his voice startled Karyn from her thoughts.

'Yes, that's true, I am,' she replied, and told him in detail about her mother.

'Well that explains a lot of things,' he remarked when she at last fell silent. 'So you are really one of us. Welcome back home, Karyn.'

The warmth in his tones made her heart seem to swell with suddenly released emotions. She had the strange feeling that she was a Greek girl who had known no other home but this sun drenched island. Was this how her mother had felt at her first meeting with her father? Karyn closed her eyes as Paul led her towards the shore, where the calm sea was glittering with the silver light of the moon. Was her mother's spirit somewhere in the ether, happy now her daughter had come to this paradise? Karyn hoped so. She felt strangely comforted as she opened her eyes and found the swishing wavelets splashing towards her feet.

'Do you swim?' Paul demanded.

'Yes,' she replied. 'I imagine the water here is more suitable than in England.'

'That you shall judge for yourself,' he said. 'If you can persuade Nerissa to leave the house we can bring her down to the beach and enjoy ourselves. It is time we all forget the past and try to pick up the broken threads of our lives.'

Karyn nodded, unable to find a suitable answer to his words. She gazed out to sea, finding it impossible to pierce the silver wall of moonlight, but she could hear the sound of a boat's oars thumping out there as some unknown fisherman propelled himself across the face of the liquid waste. There was also the distant sound of a motor boat, and it sounded suddenly urgent as the engine was opened wide. The raw noise of the powerful motor throbbed in the surrounding stillness, until there was a rending, splintering sound, punctuated by a thin, hoarse cry of fright which trailed away.

'What was that?' Karyn clutched at Paul's arm in sudden fear. A coldness filtered into her breast as she tried to see far out in the direction of the noise. The motor boat was racing away, and suddenly she caught a glimpse of a high bow wave speeding away from the shore. A light glinted momentarily, and disappeared so quickly she thought she had imagined it. She realized that Paul was standing very stiffly at her side, his head canted to one side, and his hand upon her elbow was clutching too tightly for her comfort. When she tried to wrench her arm free he stirred himself as if awakening from deep slumber, and she heard him sigh. The sound of the receding motor boat was almost gone now.

'That was a happening, Karyn,' he said huskily.

'A happening?' she demanded. 'What does that mean?'

'I couldn't tell you.' His teeth glinted in a worried grin. 'Albania is just across there, and it is shut off from us and the rest of the world. On occasion there is trouble out there in the straits, and it is wiser for one to ignore the sounds and the sights. Come, we had better return to the house. It's a long climb, and no doubt you are feeling tired after your journey. I should have had more consideration and saved the excursion down here until you'd had a chance of settling down.'

He took her arm and started hurrying her back to the cliff path, but Karyn heard a muted sound coming from the sea. Her heart seemed to miss a beat as she recognized it for a man's cry, weak and lonely and sounding remote and already out of this world.

She pulled away from him and faced the water, her ears strained for a repeat of the cry, and he took her arm again and began leading her away.

'It is none of our business,' he said gruffly. 'Please believe me when I tell you that it is better not to listen to the sounds that come on the breeze.'

'But that was a man calling for help!' Karyn protested. 'It sounded to me as if the motor boat ran down the rowing boat. That man must be floundering in the water, probably hurt and drowning.'

'And he would be drowned and under the surface before I could launch a boat and get under way,' Paul said. 'I doubt if we could find him even if we got out there in time. Come away, and I'll report the matter to the police if that will ease your mind. Please believe me when I tell you that this really is none of our business.'

Karyn strained her ears, but failed to pick up any sound above the sighing of the warm breeze and the gentle splashing of the waves. Reluctantly she allowed herself to be led from the beach, but her mind was in a turmoil as she ascended the cliff path with Paul at her side. She remained silent, trying to work out for herself what those strange noises had meant, and she was cold inside, as if a sliver of ice had been plunged into her heart. Shock filled her, and not the least of it was caused by Paul's attitude towards the incident. But right then she was too bemused to be able to think clearly, and she offered no comment and no resistance to his determined insistence to get off the beach. It was later when her mind really started protesting.

4

When they were at length standing on the *piazza*, Karyn was breathless. The lanternlight showed her Paul's face, grave, worried and indecisive. She gazed down into the brightness that was the surface of the water far below, and wondered if a man had died there amidst all the wonder of the romantic moonlight.

'The police!' she gasped. 'Hadn't you better call them, Paul?'

'Of course. Will you excuse me for a moment? I'll ring Inspector Zoulas. But I'm afraid there's little he or anyone can do. Please don't get upset over this, Karyn. I assure you that we are powerless to act in any way. We couldn't have saved that man, no matter what we did.'

'How do you know? The attempt should have been made.' Karyn spoke tonelessly, mentally struggling against the shock that tried to fill her mind.

'Karyn.' He came close and put his hands upon her slim shoulders, staring deeply into her eyes, his face intent, bold in the moonlight. 'How can I make you understand that this is not England? There are incidents taking place around this island and in these waters that have no counterpart in the life which you know. There is intrigue, smuggling, fugitives from behind the Iron Curtain? Men go out into the straits at night knowing that there is a mischance of not coming back. What they do is their business, and it is not right for any outsider to interfere. You must understand that this beautiful island of ours has its darker side. But I will ring the Inspector if it will make you feel any easier.'

He stared at her for a moment, but Karyn did not change her intent expression. Then he sighed and allowed his arms to fall to his sides. His eyes narrowed and he turned away, and Karyn saw his shoulders had slumped a little. She followed him at a distance across the *piazza* and stood in the shadows, eavesdropping while he made a telephone call. He certainly spoke to someone and gave details of what they had heard down there on the beach, but Karyn had no assurance that a policeman was at the other end of the line. She moved away as he came back into the open, and there was relief in his tones when he spoke to her.

'Would you like a drink?' he demanded. 'Then perhaps you will go to bed. It must have been a very tiring day for you. We are all strangers, and this is a strange land. I know the feeling that must be inside you now. It is not a nice one. You have the idea that you belong neither here nor in England. But I think a very few days will convince you that everything is all right.'

He brought a glass to Karyn, and stood beside her while she drank. He sipped thoughtfully from a tall glass, and Karyn could sense an awkwardness in the atmosphere. When she had finished her drink he was ready to take the glass.

'Thank you,' she said softly. 'I am grateful for your consideration. Now I will go to bed.'

'And I shall see you in the morning,' he retorted. 'Thank you for what you have done already. I feel confident that Nerissa will make great progress in your care. I am sorry about what you heard down there on the beach, and I hope it won't shatter your illusions. Goodnight, Karyn.'

'Goodnight, Paul,' she replied, and took with her as she went up to her room a picture of his face in the moonlight, composed but relaxed, relieved but filled with worry. She sighed heavily as she closed her door and switched on the light. She was filled with a baffling mixture of feelings that could not be sorted out by her tired and still shocked brain. Thinking of what had happened out at sea, she crossed to the window and peered out, staring down into the heavy shadows that guarded the cliff path.

Something moved down there in the deceptive moonlight, and Karyn caught her breath, then hurried to switch off the light. When she returned to the window her eyes were almost blind by the sudden switch in extremes. She stared downwards, and slowly her sight returned. But search as she might, she failed to see further movement anywhere along the cliff face. She sighed, wondering if the shock of the incident had started her imagination into playing tricks. Then she saw a tiny pinprick of light close to the water's edge. She bated her breath as she surveyed the area. Were the police down there already, checking out Paul's report? She set her teeth into her bottom lip as tension gripped her. She was too high to hear anything, but there seemed to be quite a lot of movement on the sands.

Tiredness nudged her mind and she sighed as she turned away from the window, undressing in the dark and preparing for bed with the aid of the silver moonlight peeping in at her. When she tumbled into bed her mind instantly began to riot, and she found herself inundated by all the impressions of the eventful day. But slowly her eyelids dropped and she began to slip under into deep slumber. She knew no more until the strong Greek sunlight poured in at the window . . .

Upon awakening, Karyn lay dreamily thinking until full consciousness returned. When she realized where she was she jerked up in bed and leaped out, hurrying to the window. She had to lift a hand to shield her eyes against the glare, and already the sun was extremely hot. She caught her breath as she stared down at the smooth, unbroken surface of the sea, and for as far as her eye could see there was deserted, glittering seascape.

The beauty of the scene robbed her mind of the grim thoughts that had lain dormant through her slumbers, but as she looked down at the strip of beach far below the house she recalled the sounds she had heard the night before. Her brows were indrawn and there was a frown between her eyes as she looked for signs of a wrecked boat. Perhaps there was even a body on the beach. She found herself holding her breath, and relaxed instantly, almost laughing aloud at her fears. She would have to take Paul's word for it that there had been nothing for them to do. It had been out of their hands, but her nurse-training had inculcated several instinctive patterns that could not be submerged by any reason, and she knew that something should have been done to investigate the mysterious incident.

Then she thought of her patient, and turned from the window to prepare to face the new day. How would she find Nerissa this morning? Would the girl have slipped back into her habitual dark mood? Karyn mentally crossed her fingers as she dressed, and hurried up the narrow flight of stairs to the attic as soon as she was presentable. She tapped at the door of the large room, and when there was no reply she opened the door and peeped into the room.

Nerissa lay asleep in the big bed, the covers half thrown off, one arm hanging over the edge of the bed. Karyn entered the room silently and moved to the foot of the bed, pausing there to study the pale, sick-looking face. The girl had been beautiful before the accident, she realized, and she hoped to restore that beauty before her job here ended.

Whether the power of her gaze disturbed the girl or not she did not know, but Nerissa stirred uneasily and slowly came awake. Karyn remained silent and still, just watching, and when the girl's eyes opened she saw slow awareness dawning in them. When their glances met Nerissa gave a start of surprise, and for a moment her face was expressionless. Karyn waited, hoping for a favourable reaction, and relief seeped into her when Nerissa smiled slowly.

'Good morning, Nerissa. I disturbed you. I'm sorry, you were in such a lovely sleep, but I don't know your routine yet, so perhaps you will forgive me just this once.'

'I've slept later than usual,' the girl replied tonelessly. 'Did you sleep well?'

'Very well, thank you. I didn't think I would, having a strange bed in a strange country, but I must have been worn out by all that happened yesterday.'

'But you will like it here?' There was a note of anxiety in the girl's voice.

'Yes. I've fallen in love with Sporveza already. I'm sure we'll get along very well, and before long you will see a difference in yourself.'

The hope that was in Karyn's voice did not communicate itself to the girl, and Karyn experienced a pang of disappointment when Nerissa slowly shook her head.

'What would you like for breakfast?' she demanded quickly, hoping to prevent the girl from slipping into her accustomed avenues of thought by changing the subject.

'Miranda knows,' Nerissa replied. 'You'll bring your breakfast up here and eat with me?'

'If you wish.' That sounded promising to Karyn and she let her own tones carry hope. 'Then this morning I'll get you down into the bathroom and let you soak in a real bath.'

'Don't bother. That will be too much trouble.'

'Not for me! Surely you don't like blanket bathing, Nerissa!'

'I don't.' The girl smiled thinly. 'All right, if you think you can manage it, but I want to come back to this room afterwards. I don't feel secure unless I'm in here with the door closed.'

'Very well. Now I'll get our breakfast.' Karyn moved to the door. 'While I'm waiting for Miranda to prepare it I shall bring up a bowl of water and wash you.'

'That's always been too much trouble,' Nerissa said.

'But not any more,' Karyn replied. 'I

have my job to do, remember.'

'I shan't forget it. I like you, Karyn. You make me realize just how lonely I have been these past months. I hope you can help me.'

'I can help you only if you want me to.' Karyn was smiling as she walked to the door. 'The fact that you want to be helped is half the battle, and admitting to yourself that you need me here with you shows that the fight is going in the right direction.'

'You make it sound as if I'm possessed by demons.'

'You are, in a way,' Karyn said, pausing in the doorway. 'Grief is a demon and so is melancholia.'

'That last one sounds very bad.'

'He's probably the worst of the whole family.' Karyn laughed. 'But I have several weapons to use against him, and in no time at all he'll be chasing out of here with his tail between his legs. Wouldn't you like to see that?'

'I'd give a lot to see it, but I think you're wasting your time.' There was a thin tone in the girl's voice, and Karyn didn't like it. 'Sometimes I feel almost normal, but most of the time I have a tight pain in the breast that feels just like a stab wound. It's caused by the pictures in my mind, and although I try to fight against it I can't find the strength. Doctor Christos has told me many times that I must fight this thing, that it is a disease just like physical illness, but I can't beat it. If I climb up out of the pit I fall back into it again.'

'We'll see about that,' Karyn promised. 'You didn't have me here before. But now I've arrived, and together we'll do what is necessary.'

She was filled with hope as she went down the stairs, and there was a smile upon her lips as she entered the kitchen. Miranda greeted her warmly, and evinced surprise at the news that Nerissa would eat breakfast.

'I haven't been able to get breakfast into her for months,' she declared. 'Thank Heaven you're here, Karyn. But Paul is going to be disappointed. He told me to prepare breakfast for the both of you on the *piazza!*

'I'm sorry about that, but my patient comes first.' Karyn breathed deeply as a thrill pierced her breast. In the back of her mind, lurking in the cover of more urgent thoughts, was the thin knowledge that Paul Stephan had made a great impact upon her, although the incident down on the shore had jangled against the smooth feeling that his company had instilled in her. 'Perhaps I may see him to apologize.'

'He's in his study. That's the second door on the left as you go out of the kitchen.' The housekeeper's dark eyes were gleaming as she studied Karyn's beautiful face.

Karyn nodded and departed, and her heart seemed to start pounding furiously as she tapped at the study door. Paul's voice bade her enter, and she opened the door and walked into the room. He was at his desk, studying some papers, but he got to his feet instantly and came forward to greet her, a thin smile upon his lips.

'Did you sleep well?' he demanded.

'Very well,' she replied, searching his face with a keen glance. He appeared to have slept badly, for there were signs of strain in his face and around his eyes. 'I came to tell you that I shall be having breakfast with Nerissa in her room.'

'Really? Is she going to have breakfast?' Hope flared in his dark eyes. 'You're certainly having a great influence upon her already. I hope you can maintain this progress. In a few weeks she will be human again.'

'Please don't expect too much,' Karyn replied. 'She may easily slip back into the rut at any time. We have to be very careful what is said to her, because the slightest word can trigger off her moods.'

'I can see that you've got a tricky job on your hands,' he said. 'If there is anything I can do to help at any time then please let me know.'

'I promise.' She smiled slowly, and changed the subject. 'Have you heard anything of what happened last night when we were down on the beach?'

'Last night?' He frowned. 'Oh! You mean the noises we heard. No. The Inspector hasn't been in touch with me, but no doubt he sent a boat out to investigate, although there was little chance by then of them finding anything.'

'What do you suppose happened?'

'I wouldn't even attempt a guess.' He shrugged, his face serious. 'Don't worry your head about it, Karyn. That sort of thing does happen quite a lot of the time.'

'That sounds like cold blooded advice,' she retorted.

'Perhaps, to ears such as yours, but if you had lived in the islands as long as I have then nothing ever comes as a surprise.'

'All right, I'll try and forget about it,' Karyn promised with a slow smile. 'Now I'd better get back to Nerissa.'

'I'd like to take you out and show you around when you have the time,' he said as she turned to the door. 'There are many beauty spots on Sporveza, and despite what you heard down on the beach last night, that spot is very peaceful and beautiful.'

'I shall look forward to the sightseeing,' Karyn said. 'But I'm afraid much of my time will be taken up with Nerissa at first. I've got to get to know her and let her find out about me. Once I've gained her confidence I shall have something to work on.'

'You're very conscientious,' he remarked, and she nodded and smiled as she left him.

Taking the tray up to Nerissa's room, Karyn found a moment for her personal thoughts, and she realized that Paul was making an impact upon her crowded mind. She was being attracted to him. That fact alone surprised her because she had never really given much time to romance. But perhaps this exotic setting had something to do with it. She nodded as she settled for that reason, and tried to control the emotions flaring up inside her.

Nerissa ate a good breakfast, and

afterwards seemed much happier. Karyn busied herself around the room, tidying and dusting, opening the windows to admit sunlight and fresh air, and she was really pleased with her progress by the time she was ready to take Nerissa down to the bathroom.

'I'll go down and prepare the bath,' she said, 'and then perhaps Miranda and I can carry you down the stairs. You're not very heavy, are you?'

'I used to weigh a great deal more,' the girl said wearily. 'It's the months of inactivity that have robbed me of my health and my figure. But more important, I've lost the will to want to get well.'

'Don't use words like those,' Karyn said. 'Remember the demons lurking in the background.'

Nerissa laughed, and for once there was no harsh sound in her tones. Karyn nodded slowly to herself. It shouldn't be too difficult to get this girl back to normal, and she couldn't help wondering about her predecessors and the methods they had employed. Nerissa had shown no improvement in their care.

With the bath ready and waiting for the girl, Karyn went in search of Miranda, and found the housekeeper talking to her husband in the kitchen. Both brown faces were deadly serious, and Karyn paused on the threshold, aware that her entrance had not been noticed. She caught something of their speech, and heard the word 'drowned' mentioned. Her ears pricked up at that, and the events of the night before returned to her.

'Sorry if I'm intruding,' she said, and both husband. and wife swung round as if startled. 'I'm ready to bring Nerissa down to the bathroom, if you'll help me carry her, Miranda.'

'Of course!' the woman exclaimed. 'This is truly a miracle, Karyn. Nerissa wouldn't let me bring her out of that room. She said she would rather die than leave it.'

'Perhaps I'm being lucky,' Karyn

replied with a smile, 'so we'd better get her into the bathroom before she can change her mind.'

Michael Orestes took his leave and Miranda accompanied Karyn up to the attic. On the way Karyn could not help mentioning what she had overheard the housekeeper saying to her husband, and when she mentioned the word 'drowned' Miranda paused on stairs and clutched at Karyn's arm. The woman's face went pale.

'It is a tragedy,' she said quickly in Greek. 'My husband's nephew was drowned last night in the bay. His boat was found shattered, half sinking, and there was no sign of the boy.'

'Did Paul tell you what we heard?' Karyn demanded.

'What was that?' The woman's dark eyes seemed to glow as she waited for Karyn to explain, and as Karyn told her about the ominous sounds they had heard down on the beach in the moonlight the woman's expression slowly tensed and grew harsh. 'So that is what happened to the boy!' she gasped. 'In the name of the Saints! Can nothing be done about those wicked men who prey upon the seas in the night?'

'What do you mean?' Karen's curiosity was aroused. 'Paul told me it was nothing to be concerned about. But you make it sound like something very different.'

'Did Paul tell you that?' Miranda demanded in shocked tones.

'He telephoned the police when we got back up here,' Karyn defended quickly. 'He spoke to an Inspector Zoulas, I believe.'

'Zoulas!' Miranda's face was ashen, and she could hardly breathe as she stared at Karyn, trying to take in the sense of what Karyn had told her.

'What's wrong, Miranda?' Karyn demanded. 'Have I said something I shouldn't?'

'No, Karyn. It's just that I am upset over the death of Michael's nephew. He was the only breadwinner in my sister-in-law's family. Michael's brother was drowned four years ago.'

'Miranda, what a tragedy!' Karyn could not keep her horror out of her tones. 'First the father and then the son! But what I heard last night couldn't have been an accident! Oh, what am I saying?' Karyn lifted a hand to her mouth and stared at the housekeeper with incredulity in her blue eyes.

'I know what you're saying, and it is something that I have suspected for a long time,' the Greek woman retorted. 'But this is no concern of yours, Karyn. Paul was right in that. Don't worry your head about it. Leave the concern to those who have lost the boy. Let us go on with your plans to bring Nerissa back to the undying love and respect of every person on the island.'

Karyn nodded slowly and they went on up to the attic, but although she said nothing more her mind was filled with perplexing questions. Was there more to this business than she knew? Why had Miranda shown such distress at the mention of Inspector Zoulas? Why hadn't

Paul shown more feeling about the possible drowning of some unknown person out there at night? The unknown turned out to be someone closely connected to Paul's own staff, but even that didn't seem to make any difference. Was Paul so cold blooded? He didn't look the type at all. Karyn felt her heart fill with misgiving as she considered it, and there was additional shock for her when she realised that she was building up a picture in her mind of Paul Stephan, a picture of a Greek knight in shining armour! But was that armour tarnished in some way? The thought filled her with disagreeable discord. Surely not! Here was the very first man she had ever felt anything for, and this upon only the second day of their meeting. Surely she hadn't picked the wrong type to become attracted to . . .

5

There were some anxious moments as they lifted Nerissa, clad only in a dressing gown, from the bed and started carrying her out of the room. Miranda and Karyn exchanged glances as they reached the door. Karyn could feel Nerissa's arms wound tightly around her neck, and the girl began to tremble as they passed through the doorway and emerged upon the stairs.

'Please . . . no!' the girl gasped in frightened tones. 'Take me back, Karyn, I implore you. I don't want to go down.'

'There's nothing to be afraid of,' Karyn soothed. 'Look, there are only a dozen stairs and then a few yards to the bathroom door. Miranda will leave us there, and she'll return to help us back up the stairs. While you're bathing I shall return to the attic and straighten the room and change the bed linen. Cling to me, Nerissa, and close your eyes. Don't even think about it.'

The girl obeyed, and her trembling ceased as they reached the bottom stair. Karyn felt easier as they went along to the bathroom, but when the door was pushed open and Nerissa saw the bath filled with steaming water she began to cry.

'The water!' she said in tremoring tones. 'I won't be able to bear it, Karyn. I haven't been in water since the accident. Please take me back up to my room.'

'Not yet, Nerissa,' Karyn encouraged. 'You don't have to go into the bath if you don't want to. You can sit upon a chair and I'll wash you. We can get you into the bath by slow degrees, as your confidence returns.' She spoke slowly and carefully, knowing that the girl's imagined terrors were very real in her distraught mind.

Relief showed upon the girl's face as they placed her upon a chair, and she sat with her legs stuck uselessly before her. Miranda glanced at Karyn, and moved quickly to the door, wanting to get away as soon as possible.

'Call me when you want to take her back to her room,' the housekeeper said, and Karyn nodded.

'Take me up now,' Nerissa pleaded, getting agitated, but Karyn closed the door of the bathroom and turned to face her patient.

'Remember that we have to fight those demons,' she said briskly. 'I'll wash you, and if you like we'll drain most of the water from the bath before lifting you into it. Tell me about yourself, Nerissa, while I'm busy.' She wanted to get the girl's mind off herself while the terror of the water was present. Nerissa was white faced, trembling, and Karyn did all she could to reassure her.

'I shan't be happy until I'm back in my room again,' Nerissa said, her teeth chattering. 'Please, Karyn, if you're my friend, take me back up.'

'Fight,' Karyn said sternly. 'What is there to be afraid of just sitting there? I'm certainly not going to harm you, and there's nothing in the room to be afraid of.' She pulled the plug from the bath and allowed most of the water to run away. The gurgling sound seemed to scare Nerissa even more, and when there was only a inch or two left Karyn replaced the plug. 'Now I'm ready for you,' she said firmly.

Nerissa looked as if she was going to resist, but Karyn undid the dressing gown and allowed it to fall away from the girl as she lifted her.

'Put your arms around my neck,' she commanded, and Nerissa reluctantly obeyed. Karyn lifted the girl bodily and put her into the bath, having to untwine Nerissa's arms before she could let go of her. 'Now what's wrong with that?' she demanded cheerfully. 'Isn't it better than a blanket bath?'

Nerissa did not answer, and Karyn began washing her. The silence was tense, but Nerissa did not object, and by degrees the girl relaxed. It was then Karyn turned on the hot water tap, and the level of the bath began to rise slowly. Karyn kept up a ceaseless chatter, saying almost anything that came into her head as the bath filled. Nerissa didn't seem to notice, but the girl kept trembling.

'What a beautiful tan you have,' Karyn said enviously. 'I certainly hope I shall be able to colour up like that before I've been here very long. Shall I get that wheel chair down from the attic when you're dressed, Nerissa? We could both do with some sunshine.'

'No!' The girl spoke harshly, and there was a glint in her dark eyes as she stared up at Karyn. 'I never go out.'

'But don't you like to look at the flowers and watch the birds?' Karyn shook her head. 'A young girl thrives on such things. I'm sure you'll feel much better for a slow walk in the sunshine.'

Nerissa did not answer, and Karyn finished bathing her.

'Pull out the plug, Nerissa.'

'Have I got to go through this every

day from now on?' Nerissa demanded, thankfully letting the water run away.

'Of course. Cleanliness is next to godliness, so they say in England.'

'That's a strange saying!' For a moment interest showed in the girl's eyes. 'You must tell me all about England.'

'I'll tell you everything you want to hear,' Karyn said with a smile, 'but you must remember that we're working together to fight this trouble of yours. I'll get you out of the bath and put the towel around you while I fetch your clean clothes.' She paused as there was a knock at the door, and Miranda entered carrying Nerissa's clothes. 'Thank you, Miranda. Now would you bring down that wheel chair I saw in the attic? Nerissa and I are going to take the air. It will give her an appetite for lunch.'

'I don't want to go outside,' Nerissa said petulantly. 'I don't have to. I haven't been outside since the accident. I never want to go outside again as long as I live.'

'That's utter nonsense. I could walk

you around while you pointed out the sights to me. Surely we aren't going to stay cooped up in the house all the time. Fresh air is a great aid in the fight against depression.'

Miranda hurried away to get the wheel chair, and as she dried and dressed the girl, Karyn wondered if she was pushing too fast. But there was no way of gauging Nerissa's readiness, and if she left it too long the novelty of having her around and doing as she was ordered would wear off and Nerissa would be back where she started.

'Now you look more like a nice young woman,' Karyn said when Nerissa was dressed. 'What a beautiful dress this is! It has a right to see the sunshine.' She opened the bathroom door and found the wheel chair standing there. Miranda had thoughtfully departed to leave Karyn alone with her charge. 'Up you come.' Karyn took up the girl and placed her in the chair. 'Now we'll go down and into the garden.'

Nerissa made no protest, but Karyn

was keeping her fingers crossed. When they reached the top of the stairs she saw Miranda waiting there, and the housekeeper took hold of one side of the chair and between them they carried it down to the ground floor.

'I shall need some sun glasses, Miranda,' Nerissa said coldly, and the housekeeper hurried away to fetch a pair. 'I don't want to go out, Karyn, but I'll do so to please you.'

As they walked towards the *piazza* Paul came out of his study, and he halted in amazement and stared at his sister and the chair. Karyn smiled, and held up a warning hand as he opened his mouth to comment upon the unusual sight, and he nodded slightly and subsided. Karyn kept going, and Nerissa sat stiff and unyielding in the chair, her hands clutching the wooden arms so tightly her knuckles showed white.

As the sunlight struck the girl she shivered, and Karyn leaned forward and pressed a tight hand upon the girl's shoulder. Miranda came up, bringing a pair of sunglasses, and Nerissa hurriedly put them on, sighing in relief as her eyes were shielded from the bright glare.

'Where would you like to go?' Karyn demanded.

'Back to my room,' came the quick reply, but Karyn ignored it and continued. They came to the gateway that led into the garden, and there was a barred gap in the parapet of the *piazza*, permitting a view of the bay and a strip of the white sands far below. Karyn paused by the bars to permit Nerissa a view of the distant scene, and the girl took one look and uttered a piercing scream. She cringed away from the view, turning her back to it, shaking the wheelchair with all the strength of her arms, and she sobbed bitterly as Karyn bent over her.

Footsteps pounded in the *piazza*, and Paul came running up as Karyn tried to comfort the girl. Nerissa was sobbing wildly, almost hysterical, and Paul was white faced as he peered down at the beach. Karyn heard him utter a gasp, and then he grasped the handle of the chair and pulled his sister back on to the *piazza*.

'That yacht down there,' he gasped quickly. 'It was the one she was on when the accident happened. She must have seen it.'

Karyn went cold as she peered down at the yacht, and then her lips thinned. She bent over the sobbing girl and tried to comfort her, but Nerissa didn't want comforting. Her cries grew louder. She seemed to be pushing herself into an hysterical fit. Paul didn't know what to do, but Karyn did, and she slapped the girl's face hard. The sobbing stopped instantly, and with a moan Nerissa slumped back into the chair and passed out.

'I'm sorry,' Karyn said, her eyes meeting Paul's. 'Perhaps I'm trying to get her to run before she can walk. Will you help me carry her to her room?'

'I thought it was too good to be true,' he said slowly, taking his sister up in his powerful arms. 'You lead the way,' he directed. 'But perhaps you are right. She won't be able to snap out of this in two or three days. She's been like it for months, and it may take as long to rescue her. Shall we call in Doctor Christos?'

'I'll have a look at her in her room,' Karyn said, leading the way. 'Getting back up there may be all that she needs.'

Karyn was dejected as she ascended the flights of stairs to the attic, but she kept a tight grip upon her feelings. It wouldn't do to let anyone see how this affected her. She could not hope that her patient would maintain cheerfulness and make progress if she herself could not show faith. When Nerissa was lying in her bed once more Paul stepped back and watched Karyn attempt to bring his sister back to consciousness. The girl was moaning, showing restlessness, and Karyn glanced at Paul as she prepared for an outburst from the girl.

Nerissa opened her eyes and stared

blankly at Karyn for a moment. The silence in the little room was oppressive. Paul came forward to stand at Karyn's shoulder, and she was keenly aware of his presence despite her preoccupation with his sister.

'How are you feeling, Nerissa?' he demanded softly. 'You gave us all a scare.'

'The yacht,' the girl said slowly, her eyes glazing slightly. 'You kept it, Paul.'

'I did,' he replied slowly. 'To you it may be an object of fearful memory, but it belonged to Father, and I kept it for a memento.'

Karyn glanced at his face and saw the seriousness in it. A pang stabbed through her and she could almost feel the pain that was in him. For a few moments his outwardly calm manner was gone, torn away by his sister's outburst. Karyn could see him as he really was, grieving and worried, his parents dead and his sister in the grip of mental stresses that threatened her whole future.

'You just close your eyes and try to

sleep, Nerissa,' Karyn said slowly. 'It was a bad shock to you, but we are making progress, aren't we?' She waited hopefully for a reply from the girl, but Nerissa closed her eyes and relaxed. Karyn watched for a few moments, with Paul intent at her side, and she thought Nerissa was too stiff to be asleep, but she turned and motioned towards the door, and Paul preceded her out of the room.

'What do you think of her?' he demanded anxiously.

'Don't worry. Perhaps the shock may turn to her advantage after all. I shall be able to tell you when I see her later. But I can see that I shall have to be extremely cautious in future, although there's no telling what may trigger her off.'

'I don't envy you the job, although I wish from the bottom of my heart that you will succeed.'

'You may rest assured that I shall do my best,' Karyn replied.

They went down the stairs, and Paul

entered his study as Karyn fetched Nerissa's wheelchair. Miranda appeared and took charge of the chair, her face showing sad disappointment at the change in Nerissa's manner.

'It was too much to hope for,' she said slowly. 'But perhaps she will change when she gets to know you better.'

'It is a setback,' Karyn admitted, 'but we're a long way from being beaten.'

Paul appeared in the doorway of the study, and he glanced at Miranda's intent face. The housekeeper sighed as she turned away, but Paul called to her.

'Would you keep an eye on Nerissa this morning, Miranda?' he demanded. 'I think she will sleep most of the time, but in any case Karyn should be shown around. I'm taking a fortnight's holiday starting now, and I want to help in any way I can.'

'Perhaps I should stay here,' Karyn said doubtfully. 'If Nerissa wakes up and starts asking for me I ought to be on hand.'

'I think it may do her good to want

you and to miss you,' the housekeeper said slyly. 'You should get to know the island before thinking seriously of settling down here with us.'

'Go and change into a dress and we'll take a run around the island in my car,' Paul said.

'Shall I put some lunch in a basket for you?' Miranda asked.

'That's a good idea.' Paul smiled slowly. 'But perhaps Karyn may think that helping me to enjoy my holiday doesn't come within the scope of her duties.'

'I'm always willing to help anywhere I can,' Karyn replied.

'Then come out with me today and let Nerissa have time to think about her progress. She may help herself to snap out of it if she's left alone.'

'I shall always be within earshot of the room,' Miranda promised. 'You don't have to worry about her.'

Karyn went up to the girl's room with a lighthearted step, and she was relieved to find Nerissa fast asleep. She stood for some moments looking down at the girl's composed face, and finally turned away with a prayer in her mind. She had to help this girl, and would if it were humanly possible.

When she had changed into a suitable pale blue dress that showed her eyes to advantage, Karyn went down to the *piazza* to find Paul waiting for her. He had changed out of his suit and now wore a white open necked shirt and grey flannels. The sleeves of the shirt were short, revealing his bronzed muscular arms, and he looked the picture of health, a gentle smile of approval on his handsome face as Karyn walked towards him.

He was watching her closely, seeing that her eyes were blue as the sea that lay so far below them. There was an eagerness in her face that made his heart turn over, and he looked away quickly, afraid that she might read something of the turmoil that was spreading in his mind.

'I thought we would drive around

while I pointed out the more beautiful sights,' he said. 'Later I would show you the village of Lanois, and then we could go into Khalmia. You saw the harbour there when you came ashore yesterday, but I expect you didn't get the chance to see much, it all being so strange.'

'You've tempted me from my patient,' Karyn replied softly. 'I hope Nerissa won't want me when she wakes up.'

'So I'm a bad influence, but perhaps there is a method in my manner.' He was smiling. 'Nerissa won't need too much of you to start with, and I can't have you getting bored and feeling homesick.'

'I shall never become homesick!' Karyn spoke with such force that he showed momentary surprise. 'I have no-one in England to care about,' she went on. 'I belong to two worlds, remember; England and Greece. Since my father died there is nothing in England to hold me. Now that I am here I think I shall remain, no matter what happens with Nerissa. If she does recover her health then I shall look for another position here.'

Miranda appeared with a picnic basket, and Paul took it from the woman, thanking her. Miranda glanced at Karyn's happy face and gleaming eyes and nodded thoughtfully to herself. Then she addressed Paul.

'Perhaps you had better not go into Lanois today,' she said thinly. 'There they will be lamenting the loss of Ari, our nephew.'

Paul's face lost its happy expression, and a host of emotions showed fleetingly before he controlled them. He glanced at Karyn, saw that her eyes were upon him, and shook his head slowly.

'It is a tragedy,' he said. 'But I knew nothing about it, Miranda. I hope you will believe that. Last night Karyn and I heard the sounds at sea that might have come from the accident Ari suffered. I told Karyn then that it would be useless to try to do anything, and I still believe that. Even if I had taken the boat out we wouldn't have found anything.'

'But there was no trouble until you permitted the fishermen to use the bay,' Miranda said.

'That is what they wanted,' Paul retorted. 'I have given them the rights they asked for. If they find those men too dangerous then they can keep away. I don't insist that they use the bay.'

Karyn listened, mystified by what was said. But she was a little relieved to hear Paul's words. She had subconsciously begun to think that in some obscure way Paul had known what was happening out at sea during the night. She had felt that he could have raised the alarm more quickly and organized a search, but now she was beginning to have second thoughts, and she felt easier as she learned a little from their conversation.

'Do you want me to forbid the fishermen to use the bay?' Paul demanded finally.

'It would keep them off the course those men use in their evil business,' Miranda retorted. 'Of course the fishermen take chances because the best fishing is in the bay. They hope to elude those power boats, but if they were forbidden to use the bay then that would settle the whole business.'

'All right.' Paul sighed heavily. 'I shall give orders and make it known that the bay is out of bounds to all islanders. It will cause a stir in other quarters, I can tell you, but I can't accept the responsibility any longer. Come along, Karyn, before my thoughts spoil the day for us.'

Karyn followed him across the *piazza* and down the steps to where his car was parked. He put the basket into the boot and helped her into the car. His face was grim as he proceeded to drive away from the house, and Karyn settled back, wanting to ask questions but not daring to. She stared at the scenery that surrounded them, and her heart ached to see such beauty.

The morning was hot, but not oppressively so. At times Karyn caught a glimpse of the sparkling turquoise sea as the road dipped and twisted around the coast. Mountains hemmed in the coastal area, and the heavy perfume of the scented *maquis* growing over the hills filled her nostrils with enchanting power. She could feel herself responding to the beauty of this island. Paul drove as if he was engrossed elsewhere, and from time to time Karyn glanced at his intent face and wondered what was filling his mind. She didn't wonder that he seemed a lonely person. The tragedy of his parents and his sister, and business worries on top of that, was enough to sour the most even of manners. But there was more in the background, she felt sure, and the incident in the bay the night before had a great bearing upon his burdens.

The car swept around a bend and there before them lay Khalmia and its beautiful harbour. Lifting herself up slightly to obtain a better view, Karyn felt her heart was touched by the sight. A ship was nosing out into the straits, looking for all the world like a boy's model, and the sea was so calm it seemed unreal, like a sea-scape painted by some skilled natural hand. A yacht was tacking slowly, taking advantage of every whim of the faint, warm breeze, and there was a thin cream of disturbed water trailing out from its sleek stern.

'What do you think of Khalmia now?' Paul demanded, and Karyn looked at his classically Grecian face. She felt a sudden urge to reach out trembling fingers and touch his black curly hair.

'It's too beautiful,' she replied. 'It's too good to be true.'

Paul smiled as he parked the open car in a patch of shade, and they left the vehicle and strolled through the alleyways to the market, where a host of good natured people swarmed around the many stalls. There were strange, spicy smells in the air, and the brightness every-where hurt Karyn's eyes. She was lost in a dream world as they looked around, and she did not see that Paul was watch-ing her closely and deriving much pleasure from her obvious happiness.

They reached the waterfront, where a low stone wall bounded the harbour. Many small boats were tied up along the quay, and men were working upon them, cleaning and repairing, mending nets and preparing for their next trip. Paul seemed to tense as they continued, and presently they came unexpectedly upon a solitary figure of an old man seated on the harbour wall. He looked as if he had sprung from the dark pages of Greek history, dressed in baggy trousers tucked into knee-boots. His coloured shirt had seen better days. There was a knotted handkerchief upon his head. His face was dark, like weathered mahogany, and the black moustachios under his hooked nose added to the fierceness of his appearance. He could have been a brigand or an old pirate, but he carried nothing more aggressive than a basket.

Paul halted when he saw the man, and Karyn paused, wondering what was occupying Paul's mind at that moment. She saw the uneasiness in him and followed the direction of his gaze, finding the old gypsy the object of his attention. She heard Paul sigh, and then he reached out a trembling hand and took hold of her arm, turning her away, almost running to get out of sight before the gypsy should see them. When they turned a corner Paul halted, and his face was pale. Karyn was breathless as she stared at him. He looked so scared she was astonished, but she said nothing. Paul tried to regain his composure as they walked on, but Karyn could tell that he was badly upset, and she wondered greatly why the sight of that solitary old man should have worried him so.'

6

They went back to the car and drove on, and now there seemed to be a difference in Paul's manner. His face was stern, and even his dark eyes had lost the gleam that shone from them before they reached the town. He drove southwards, and Karyn lost herself again in the beauty of the scenery. Whenever they had a glimpse of the sea she marvelled at its brightness, and shivered when she recalled the depressing weather she had left behind in England. The two countries seemed to be in different worlds.

Paul turned into a narrow road that led to the cliffs overlooking a small cove. He parked the car and fetched the hamper from the boot. Leading the way, he took Karyn down to the beach. They went down to the water's edge and stood facing the soft sea breeze, and Karyn enjoyed its gentle caress against her hot face. Far out upon the placid waters a small fishing boat lay motionless, as if trapped upon plate glass, and Karyn was reminded of the grim incident which had occurred the previous night. Despite the beauty on this island there was a darker side, and she shivered as she tried to imagine how it affected Paul.

They ate on the beach, and Karyn enjoyed every moment of their stay. She loved Paul's company, for he had recovered somewhat from his fear in the town and was more like his real self, gentle, considerate and good fun to be with. Later they went back to the car and resumed their tour of the island.

By the time they had to return to the house Karyn was tired. The day had been long and all the new sights and impressions to be assimilated were thronging her brain. Beneath it all was worry of the kind she had never experienced before. When they reached the house and she waited for Paul to get the hamper from the boot she found herself analysing the day, and she knew that she had fallen beneath his spell. There was something in his eyes, his manner, that captivated her. Mere attraction couldn't explain it. She felt as if she had been waiting all her life just to meet him, and now that each knew the other existed it seemed that Nature was making her aware that this man was right for her.

She narrowed her eyes as she caught sight of his expression. It was one of his unguarded moments, and his face was serious, his dark eyes brooding. Then he looked up and saw her watching, and the smile returned and his whole manner changed. As he came towards her he nodded slowly.

'Thank you for putting up with me today,' he said. 'I needed a change like that to lift me out of the rut. You must be thinking that we Stephans are very strange people.'

'Certainly not,' Karyn replied. 'I've thoroughly enjoyed myself. It was most kind of you to take me around.'

'I hope we may go out together again,' he said eagerly. 'I hope Nerissa won't take up too much of your time.'

'I'd better go and see her right away,' Karyn replied. 'But thank you again for such a wonderful day.'

'It's my holiday.' He was smiling. 'I shall be looking for you tomorrow.'

'Perhaps we could induce Nerissa to come out with us in the car,' she suggested. 'What she needs is some diversion that will take her completely out of herself.'

'Talk to her about it,' he said eagerly. 'Then I shan't have to spend the next two weeks mainly on my own.'

Karyn nodded and smiled, and they entered the house. Paul took the hamper into the kitchen and Karyn hurried up the stairs to the attic. She paused outside the door, her heart thumping more from the excitement of the day than the exercise of running up the stairs. Then she tapped at the door and entered the room, looking eagerly at Nerissa's face when she saw the girl, wondering if the incident of the morning had thrown the girl back a retrogressive step.

Nerissa lay in bed staring blankly at the ceiling. She did not stir when Karyn entered the room, and gave no indication of having seen her when Karyn sat down at the side of the bed.

'Hello, Nerissa,' Karyn said softly. 'How are you feeling now?'

There was no reply, and Karyn stared intently at the girl's face. Nerissa was awake, her pretty face set sullenly, and her eyes were fixed determinedly in the distance.

'Nerissa, please speak to me.'

The girl's head came slowly around until her dark eyes were staring at Karyn. The richly curved lips parted, but the girl did not speak. Karyn watched her, wondering what was passing through the distraught mind. She sighed slowly, wondering if she had used the wrong approach in the first place.

'You've been out enjoying yourself

the whole day,' the girl accused suddenly.

'Yes, I have. It was wonderful. I think Sporveza is the most beautiful place I have ever seen. But there's no need for you to sound envious, Nerissa. I suggested to Paul that we take you out tomorrow. He's on holiday for the next two weeks and doesn't know what to do with himself.'

'I don't want to go out,' the girl said firmly.

'All right, you don't have to. I'm sorry for that incident this morning. But I just thought that you would rather get out and see what's happening on the island. There's no future in this narrow prison of a world that you've made for yourself in this room. You have so much on your mind that you ought to try and forget some of it. By staying isolated up here you're nurturing this illness in your mind instead of fighting it. We agreed yesterday that we would fight, didn't we? You haven't given up so soon, have you?'

'It's too difficult,' the girl said slowly. 'No matter where I look when I'm out of this room I can see signs of my parents. I'd rather stay here and try to forget in my own way.'

'But you're not trying to forget,' Karyn said strongly. 'All you want to do is remember. That's why you're staying up here. It's easier to remember when there are no outside distractions.'

'That's not true! I want to forget it all. I want to come back to life.'

'Then I'll tell Paul that you will go with us tomorrow,' Karyn said. 'I'll get you dressed up and you can sit in the back of the car.'

'I'll think about it tonight,' Nerissa told her coldly. 'Where did you go today?'

'Would you like an account of the whole day?' Karyn smiled as she settled herself by the girl's side, and she launched into a graphic description of her outing with Paul. Nerissa listened in silence, and when Karyn had finished the girl's eyes were gleaming.

'What do you think of Paul?' she asked suddenly.

'I think he's very nice,' Karyn said slowly, watching the girl's face for expression. 'He's suffering badly, Nerissa. You could help him a lot by taking more interest in what he does. He's running the business now, and it's a very lonely job. He could help you, too. There's only the two of you left, and you are both children of your parents. If you miss your parents so much then surely you want to do as they would have wished. Think of your mother, Nerissa, and tell me if she would be happy knowing that you shut yourself away like this.'

'Don't,' the girl groaned, covering her ears with her hands. 'I can't bear to listen to you.'

'I'll go and see if Miranda has prepared your tea,' Karyn said, and she hurried from the room, knowing that she had been cruel to make the girl think of what had happened. But she was trying to get Nerissa to think in a positive way, and that was very much different to the frame of mind the girl herself had cultivated.

The housekeeper was sad, and Karyn felt a pang of remorse when she thought of the tragedy which had taken place the night before. It had happened while she stood enraptured upon the shore. A young fisherman had lost his life in the silvery moonlight, and the circumstances of his death were very odd. Karyn thought of Paul and the reaction which sight of the old gypsy had brought to him. Was there any connection with Paul's fear, which had been very real for a short time, and the mysterious disappearance of Miranda's nephew?

'You have enjoyed yourself today, Karyn,' Miranda said wisely.

'It has been a wonderful day,' Karyn agreed. 'And I'm relieved to find Nerissa in such an easy state of mind. I was afraid that this morning's incident would have retarded her recovery, but she seems in good spirits. I'm keeping my fingers crossed that we shall be able to get her to take a ride in the car with us tomorrow.'

'So that's the way it is to be!' Miranda stared at her with joy in her brown eyes, and Karyn smiled slowly as she recognized the woman's drift.

'Anything to make Nerissa happy,' Karyn said slowly.

'And I agree with that,' Miranda told her. 'But tell me about your day. Where did you go and what did you see?'

'There was an old gypsy in Khalmia,' Karyn said hesitantly. 'Paul was upset when he saw him, and there was fear in him for a long time afterwards. Can you tell me why?'

'You saw Loukas Benassis?' Miranda made no attempt to conceal the worry which came to her face.

'Why should Paul be afraid?' Karyn questioned. 'What is wrong in these waters, Miranda?'

'It is nothing that has any part in this modern age,' the housekeeper said in reply. 'You know our history spans many centuries. We had a civilization before England came out of her dark ages. But you are half Greek, Karyn, and perhaps you can sense a part of what I mean. Your mother will have passed on to you some of her instincts. I know you have a deep feeling for us and our country. I saw it in your face the first time I met you. Yet there is much that you cannot even guess at, and it would be better for you not to concern yourself with what might be going on in these parts.'

'Paul said just about the same thing,' Karyn replied. 'Of course it is none of my business, but your husband's nephew disappeared from his boat, which was found smashed and sinking. I find it hard not to think that this is all to do with activities that are outside the law. Paul spoke to an Inspector Zoulas, and when I mentioned it to you I had the feeling that you disapproved. My curiosity is aroused, Miranda. Is there anything you can tell me? Paul isn't mixed up in anything like that, is he?

You warned him not to go into Lanios today. Why? Is there someone there who might want to harm him ?'

'It is better not to talk of these things, Karyn. Kill your curiosity before it gets the better of you. Take an interest in Paul by all means. He has a great need for someone like you to help him. When he advertised for a nurse for Nerissa he should have included his name with hers. They both need help, although Paul only to a lesser degree.'

'And you won't tell me what kind of help he needs,' Karyn said. 'That's tying my hands, Miranda.'

'I can't help you any more, Karyn,' the housekeeper replied. 'Perhaps you can do more good in your ignorance of the situation.'

Karyn suppressed a sigh when she realized that she wouldn't learn any more from Miranda. She left the kitchen while waiting for Nerissa's meal, and went out to the *piazza*, half hoping to see Paul there, but there was no sign of him. She stood at the parapet and stared down at the sea and the beach, her mind reflecting upon the strange events of the past day. What was happening here on this beautiful island? How did it affect Paul?

She realized that she was becoming increasingly concerned about Paul, and wondered what was in the back of her mind. A restlessness seized her and she paced the *piazza*. She didn't halt until Miranda came to tell her Nerissa's meal was ready.

Going up to the attic, Karyn began to wish that time would pass. If a month could slip suddenly away she would be in a better position to judge her impressions. If Nerissa was going to recover then in a month her progress should be marked. Her impatience was strange, and Karyn shook her head in wonderment as she went into the attic to see Nerissa.

The girl ate her meal, but spoke very little. She was occupied with deep thoughts, and Karyn hoped she was thinking constructively.

'Are you taking a liking to Paul?' Nerissa demanded suddenly.

'Paul?' Karyn's heart seemed to miss a beat as she said the name. 'I do like him! He's a very fine man.'

'Could you love him?' the girl persisted.

'I don't know. We're still strangers, Nerissa. But that's an odd question. What are you thinking?'

'Paul needs a wife,' the girl said slowly. 'He's got everything he needs except a wife. But the girl he should marry will have to be almost an angel, and you're the first one I've ever met.'

'An angel?' Karyn laughed musically, but there was a warmth in her heart that boosted her confidence. If she was winning over this girl then there was a good chance for her. 'I'm far from being an angel, Nerissa. I do my best, of course, but that isn't good enough some of the time. Look at the mistake I made with you this morning. I should have realized that sight of the yacht would upset you.'

'But you didn't know it was out there,' the girl protested.

'I should have checked. The reason why you want to stay in this room is because you're afraid of seeing anything connected with the past. I knew that, and yet I didn't check that there was nothing around that would give you offence.'

'I promise to be better tomorrow,' Nerissa said. 'If you promise you'll try and fall in love with Paul then I'll make an extra effort to get well.'

'I'll agree to anything that will help you get on your feet,' Karyn replied, her cheeks reddening. 'But I have a feeling that you've got the easiest part of the bargain. Paul seems to me to be self sufficient. Any girl would have an impossible task to attract him.'

'Is that what you've decided about him?' Nerissa shook her head in wonder. 'Paul isn't a bit like that really. I expect the accident changed him, but if it did then he's as much in need of your help as I am.'

'But he hasn't asked for help.'

'I didn't,' came the spirited reply. 'Paul decided that I needed help and you arrived, so if I decide that he needs help then it's only fair that I do for him what he's done for me.'

'That's right.' Karyn was filled with new hope at the girl's words. The most important thing for her to accomplish was to make Nerissa start thinking beyond herself. Until the girl could get her mind off her own narrow circle nothing would work for her. Now here she was suggesting that her brother needed help. Perhaps that seemingly unfortunate incident of the morning was having the desired effect.

'Will you promise to fall in love with Paul?' There was such anxiety in the girl's tones that Karyn felt emotion rise in her breast.

'If you promise to go along with my every suggestion,' she replied.

'Then we'll make a bargain on it.' Nerissa held out her slim hand and Karyn clasped it thankfully. For a moment they stared into each other's eyes, and Karyn could see the girl was deadly serious. Her grip was strong. Gone was her listlessness. This was the very situation Karyn had been hoping to achieve, and the girl had decided it for herself.

'We'll both make an immediate start,' Karyn said. 'If I get the chance I'll see Paul this evening and start working my angelic ways upon him. Have you any special instructions for the way I should go about it? You know your brother far better than I.'

'No.' Nerissa spoke sharply. 'I have no authority on which to base advice of that nature. You must follow your own natural instincts. But I will do as you say with regard to myself because you're qualified to make the decisions.'

'Good. Now we have something to work from. Come and finish your meal.'

'You can leave me alone because I want to think,' Nerissa replied. 'But before you go will you tell me something?'

'Anything.'

'Do you think it is true that the

reason I cannot walk is because subconsciously I don't want to?'

'There's nothing physicaly wrong with you, Nerissa. I expect Doctor Christos was correct in saying that the shock of the accident has caused this paralysis. We're going to start working on that. Tomorrow I shall start massage treatment, and you'll be surprised at the effect that may have upon you. Now that you feel you want to get well we should get some good results.'

'If I do get better then it will be because you took the trouble to show me how wrong I am to lie here wasting my time. But leave me now, Karyn. I wish to think.'

Karyn nodded and departed, and her heart beat hopefully as she went down to the kitchen. But what a way to gain the co-operation of her patient! She smiled slowly. She had to use any means at her disposal, and pretending to fall in love with Paul Stephan would not be too difficult. She thought of him as she went in search of Miranda. The day spent with him had given her some knowledge of him, she found that she was attracted to him, but she didn't for a moment think that he could ever feel the same way about her.

'Well?' Miranda demanded. 'How is she? Has this morning's trouble upset her? Is she back where she started?'

'No!' Karyn explained what had passed between her and Nerissa, and Miranda nodded knowingly.

'So she has risen to it!' The housekeeper was smiling. 'I put it to her today,' she explained. 'I realized that you would need help in getting Nerissa into the right frame of mind. It should have been obvious to me before you arrived that the best way to cure her was to get her thinking of someone else. That's what you're doing, isn't it Karyn?'

'Yes. If she can occupy herself with other people's problems she will have won the first and hardest battle.'

'And you are going to pretend to fall in love with Paul?'

141

'I'm going to pretend anything in order to get that girl on her feet,' Karyn declared emphatically.

Miranda smiled as she nodded. 'I've told you that he needs help just like Nerissa,' she said. 'You can count on me to help in any way I can.'

Karyn was about to answer when the kitchen door opened and Paul looked in. He smiled when he saw her, and motioned for her to follow him. When they stood on the *piazza* he faced her with a sigh.

'Karyn, I have to go out this evening, so you will have to dine alone. But I won't be long. When I come back may I take you for a walk along the cliffs? That's if you're not too tired from the day's activities.'

'I'd love to go with you,' she said instantly. 'I'll be waiting for your return.'

He eyed her intently for a moment, and his dark eyes gleamed. Karyn studied him with the knowledge that she liked him in the forefront of her mind. Her pulses started pounding and she had to avert her gaze. The strangest emotions began to flare up inside her. She suddenly felt confused, and her brain froze. An awkward feeling seized her and she felt the urge to say something, to get him talking in the hope that he wouldn't notice her growing self-consciousness.

'I've made a bargain with Nerissa,' she said almost frantically. Then she told him what had transpired between her and the girl, and saw interest flare up in his eyes.

'Well that's something,' he retorted with a crooked smile. 'But we'll have to work at this pretence, won't we? Nerissa is a very perceptive girl, and she may see through any fabrication you make. I've already told you that I will do anything to help, so perhaps we'd better go along with her whims. If it helps her it will be worth it. But she's wrong in supposing that I need help of any kind. I don't. I'm quite busy with all that I have to do, although I won't deny that I'm lonely and depressed at times. It would be wrong for me to believe otherwise. However, here comes Miranda, and I know she tells Nerissa everything that happens around the house. So this is a good chance for us to start making believe.'

Before Karyn realized what he was doing she was in his arms and his mouth was pressing against her. She instinctively struggled against him for a moment, but then the magic of his lips overpowered her and she didn't care that Miranda was coming. All to the good, she thought as she closed her eyes, and the lingering kiss set the seal upon her enchantment. After this, she told herself remotely, life would never be the same . . .

7

After Paul had gone about his business that evening, Karyn wandered through the big old house, her mind bathed in dreams. She could still feel the pressure of his mouth against hers, and the feelings stirred up inside her at their contact would not subside. She seemed to be walking on air, and even the memory of Miranda smiling happily at their backs while Paul kissed her did not lessen her happiness. But there was a strong, disturbing thought in the back of her mind. Where did Paul fit into all the mysterious happenings that were occurring around Sporveza?

The evening was warm and she didn't expect Paul back for at least another hour. Nerissa had settled down happily to sleep, and Karyn went to the *piazza* and stood staring down at the sea. The water looked inviting, and she suddenly felt the desire to bathe in its lucid depths. She went in search of Miranda, and found the woman in the kitchen with her husband.

Michael Orestes got to his feet at Karyn's entrance, and she noticed that he was showing anxiety in his rugged brown face. But filled with her own wonderful feelings, Karyn was out of this world. She asked Miranda if there was such a thing as a bathing suit in the house, and the housekeeper fetched her one of Nerissa's.

'Be careful down there,' Michael Orestes said in his thick tones.

'Don't frighten the girl,' Miranda reproved, wrapping the bathing suit in a huge beach towel. 'There's nothing to be afraid of in the cove.'

'I'm not trying to frighten her,' he protested sourly. 'I am warning her to be careful. The path down the cliffs is a bit dangerous, as well you know, and Karyn is a stranger here. Apart from that there are some tricky currents in the cove.'

146

'But Karyn will not venture out that far,' Miranda said.

'She won't now that she's been warned,' her husband replied with a grin at Karyn.

'I won't go too far in,' Karyn said. 'I just want to get the feel of the water. Is it as warm as it looks?'

'Every bit of it,' Miranda said. 'If I wasn't so busy here I'd go with you, but I shall be watching you from time to time from the *piazza*, Karyn. Don't stay too long for this first time, will you?'

'I promise.' Karyn could feel the tug of desire in her. She took her leave of them and went through the garden to the cliff path, recalling how she had negotiated it with Paul in the moonlight the evening before. The path seemed dangerous, she thought as she started descending, but it was safe enough if one stayed away from the edge.

Down on the beach she changed into the bathing suit among the pines growing close by and then ran across the bright sand to the water. Tiny wavelets caressed the beach, and when she tested the water she found it surprisingly warm. Without further ado she waded in and dived deeply, closing her eyes in pleasure as she surged into the depths. Bathing in England had never been like this, she thought as she surfaced and trod water. She stared around, searching the line of the cliffs, taking in the beautiful scene that was even now beginning to grow indistinct with the onset of evening. She saw the Stephan house high up on the very edge of the sheer drop, caught a glimpse of the parapet around the *piazza*, and felt strangely comforted by the thought that Miranda would be able to see her down here.

Karyn began to swim parallel to the shore, striking out cleanly and strongly, moving towards the anchored yacht that had seen the tragedy which claimed Nerisa's parents. She saw a boathouse half hidden among the trees on the shore, and there was a small chalet nearby. It was a private beach, Karyn remembered, and she wondered at the sort of life that

Nerissa must have led before the accident. Surely the girl missed all of that!

When she reached the yacht she swam around it, sensing the atmosphere about it. She saw the rocks close in where the vessel had struck during the storm, and when she examined the bows closely she saw where repairs had been carried out. She shivered as she imagined the dreadful accident. No wonder Nerissa had been so badly shocked! It was a wonder the girl hadn't completely lost her reason. Karyn struck for the shore and waded on to the beach, standing straight and slim in the gathering gloom. It was time to go back to the house! She felt dejected for some unknown reason as she started walking through the sand.

There was a deep inlet before the boathouse, which had obviously been made for the purpose of making the launching of the Stephan craft that much easier, and Karyn paused to peer down into the apparently deep water. The last of the sunlight was piercing the depths, lighting up a shoal of small fish nibbling and darting about in their own private sea, and Karyn's probing eyes caught the glint of metal down there among the bunches of weed that clung obdurately to the small rounded rocks. The straying beams of sunlight were searching the gloomy hollows among the rocks as if bidding them adieu for another day and, striking bright metal, caused it to glint refractedly in the gentle swell that moved the weed continuously.

The glint attracted Karyn's eyes instantly, and she frowned as her gaze tried to follow the darker outline of something trapped down there among the rocks. She bent forward and pushed her face close to the water to reduce the glare, and saw immediately that what she thought was just brown weed was in fact the cloth of a man's trousers. When she realized that there were legs in those trousers she chilled and gasped, drawing back in shock, and the whole outline of the body down there became apparent, as if her shock had caused scales to fall from her eyes.

The glinting metal which had first attracted her eyes was part of a dagger blade, the point being buried in the dead man's back between the shoulders. The brassy handle of the dagger was projecting from the limp flesh. Karyn sighed deeply as she guessed this would be the body of the missing fisherman — Michael Orestes' nephew — and the knowledge that she had heard the grim sounds accompanying this man's death made Karyn feel sick.

She got to her feet and peered around. She was alone down here, and there were no boats out on the water, except the lonely yacht that had been the vehicle of tragedy for Nerissa. Looking into the depths again, as if unable to believe the evidence of her eyes, Karyn saw the dark head of the dead man, the face which already was suffering the ravages of the water and sea-creatures. She stumbled away, stifling a cry, and hurried back to the spot where she had left her clothes.

The sun was going now, cut off from the beach by the high cliffs, and there seemed a hostile atmosphere around Karyn as she dressed hurriedly. Her hands trembled as she pulled on her clothes, and then she started up the cliff path as fast as she could move. She was soon breathless, and had to pause for relief. The path was steep and treacherous, and shadows were crawling into the deep places. The sea was beginning to look secretive, and until the moon rose it would be cloaked in darkness. Thinking of what lay below in the inlet, Karyn was spurred on again, and she hurried on, gasping for breath, intent upon returning to the house.

By the time she reached the *piazza* she was almost exhausted, and she paused for a moment in the shadows of a large stone pot on the very edge of the parapet. There was a pounding in her ears, and her breathing was ragged. The evening was almost completely dark now, and she spotted the red glow of a cigarette at the far end of the *piazza*.

Paul, she thought, and was about to start forward when she heard the voices. She halted in midstride, warned by the harsh tones, and breathed shallowly through her mouth as she tried to regain her composure.

'You're a fool, Paul,' she heard a man's voice say. 'How many times do I have to tell you that there is no need for alarm? Everything is going according to plan, and if you will only do what I ask you there's no need to concern yourself about any of the details.'

'You call what happened to Ari last night just a detail?' Paul sounded angry, and his tones were low, filled with tension.

'Paul, I swear that we had nothing to do with that. Ari must have run afoul of those night runners across the straits. I tell you there is no need for violence in our business.'

'You may keep your business to yourself, Lanni.' Paul sounded decisive. 'My father never mixed with your kind, and I'm sure I never shall. I'm not the type. My business as it is satisfies me. What more can I do? I let the fishermen use the bay, but that, it seems, was wrong, so I've withdrawn the liberty. I can't please anyone!' His tones deepened as anger filled him. 'My servant's nephew disappeared last night, Lanni, and I'm not convinced that your men are innocent.'

A tall figure moved by the parapet, and the red glow of the cigarette described a bright arc through the night as it was flicked away into the deep space beyond the bulging cliff.

'You know my business is a part of our history,' the stranger said. 'The island men have always traded without bar or prohibition. The Iron Curtain has added to the value of some of our merchandise. We may as well reap the benefit of the prices. If we don't supply the needs then someone else will take over. We wouldn't stop it by ceasing to operate. But we need to have the fishermen in the bay, Paul. With all the small boats around we have a better chance of operating among them. Without their cover we would soon fall victim to those speed boats.'

'That's exactly what happened to Ari last night,' Paul said.

Karyn thought of the lifeless body in the water, and shuddered as she recalled the knife handle protruding from the man's back. She caught her breath and went forward on to the *piazza*, calling Paul's name urgently.

'Over here, Karyn,' he said quickly, and materialized from the gloom. 'What's wrong? Where have you been?'

Karyn explained in low, flat tones that gave no indication of her feelings. She watched the tall stranger standing just beyond Paul as she spoke, but it was too dark for her to see his features.

'Ari?' The stranger said as Karyn finished her account.

'Who else?' Paul demanded. 'Wait here, Karyn. I must call Inspector Zoulas and report this. There was a knife in his back, you say?'

'Yes!' Karyn felt faint as she relaxed.

Now that the onus of reporting her find was removed from her she was assailed by reaction, and her knees were trembling as she walked to the table and sat down. The lanterns were not yet alight, and she was glad of the shadows. Paul introduced the stranger as Lanni Marfissa, and he came forward to take her hand briefly.

'Pour her a drink, Lanni,' Paul said quickly as he went to the telephone. 'It must have been quite a shock for her.'

Karyn took the drink and thanked the man. Marfissa sat down opposite her, his teeth gleaming a little as he smiled. Beyond seeing that he was dark skinned and wore a thick black moustache, Karyn could tell nothing else about him.

'So you're Nerissa's English nurse!' he said by way of opening a conversation. 'How is the girl?'

'I think she will make good progress in the near future,' Karyn replied. She judged by his tones that he was not an old man. 'I suppose you know her well!'

'I used to. Now nobody knows her at all. I would have married her if she had not fallen in love with Nikos Ellas.'

'She mentioned him to me. What happened to him? He doesn't still call on her, does he?'

'Not Nikos. If a girl cannot get out to meet him then he doesn't want to know her. I would have cut off my right arm to have the chances he got, but that's the way of it in this world. Now he doesn't want Nerissa, and I don't get the chance.'

'Are you a good friend of hers?' Karyn demanded.

'I've known her since we were children. But that doesn't signify a thing. Nerissa is a strange girl, and no doubt the accident has made her even more strange.'

'Mentally, she's undamaged,' Karyn defended.

'But her legs. They were broken, but they have healed. Yet she cannot walk.'

'It is a condition of the mind, but that is not to say she has a mental disability.

She needs help, but I'm willing to stake my reputation on the fact that within a very short time she will be normal again.'

'If you are that certain then I will believe you!' He laughed, and half turned as Miranda came on to the *piazza* to light the lanterns.

As the light flared Karyn got her first look at him, and she was impressed by his attractive features. He was dark and handsome, with a flowing moustache that seemed to give him a devil-may-care manner. His dark eyes glinted in the lights, and he leaned forward boldly to look at her. But Karyn's attention was taken by Miranda. The housekeeper came to the table and stared down at her.

'Karyn, the man in the water, can you describe him?'

'I'm sorry, Miranda, but I can't.' Karyn suppressed a shudder. 'He was down a long way, and the water distorted his features.'

'How was he dressed?' Marfissa demanded gently.

'Brown trousers. That's all I noticed.

His shirt was light coloured.'

'Ari!' Miranda spoke the name in a choking voice, and Karyn got to her feet and slid an arm around the woman's plump shoulders. She thought Miranda was going to cry, but the housekeeper shook her head slowly and returned to the house. Karyn sat down again, wondering what was keeping Paul, and she recalled the reaction Miranda had shown at the mention of Inspector Zoulas. She looked at Marfissa, who seemed completely at ease now, his conversation with Paul probably forgotten, and Karyn took an instinctive dislike to this man because he had apparently been trying to persuade Paul to join in some dubious business venture. From what she had overheard, Karyn had no doubt that Marifissa was actively engaged in smuggling.

'Who is Inspector Zoulas?' she asked suddenly.

'Zoulas?' Marifissa picked up his glass and drank slowly from it. His dark eyes studied Karyn's intent face from beyond the wide rim of the glass. 'He's the senior policeman on the island.'

'Miranda doesn't like him!'

'None of the islanders do! Zoulas comes from Athens. He's an outsider! He's been here about three years, and it will take him another twenty to get himself accepted here. His predecessor was a local man, and for some obscure reason Zoulas is blamed for his departure, although that is utter nonsense. But that is the way the minds of the island folk work.'

So there was nothing more sinister about Inspector Zoulas than the fact that he had, in the minds of the islanders, usurped a local man. Karyn sighed her relief as she found some of her fears about Paul's part in all these darker activities fading into obscurity. And on top of that Paul had turned down this man's offer of business. She breathed deeply, feeling the tension seeping out of her, and then Paul came back, his face pale and grim in the lanternlight.

'You'd better get away from here,

Lanni,' he said to Marfissi. 'Zoulas will be here very shortly. I don't want him to know that you've been here.'

'That's not saying much for me,' Marfissa said gently, his eyes upon Karyn's face. 'What will your English nurse think of me?'

'Nothing at all, if she has any sense,' Paul remarked lightly, but there was a curious glint in his dark eyes. 'I would be obliged if you would return to Khalmia by way of the back road.'

'Anything to oblige.' Lanni Marfissa got to his feet, and although Paul was tall, Karyn saw that the visitor towered over him by several inches. 'I am most happy to have met you, Miss Gregory. I hope it will be my good fortune to meet you again. Now goodnight.'

'Goodnight,' Karyn retorted, and she relaxed as Paul escorted Marfissa away.

When Paul returned he came to the table and sat down, facing Karyn, staring into her face and reaching across the table to take hold of one of her hands in a gentle grip.

'I am so sorry you've had such a shock,' he said. 'Are you feeling all right? The inspector will be here soon, and no doubt he will want to question you about your discovery. Then we shall have to go down there to recover the body. Are you certain it was a knife you saw in this man's back?'

'Positive,' Karyn replied. 'It was the sun glinting upon the dagger that attracted my attention in the first place.'

'You must have very strong nerves,' he went on. 'Many girls would have fled in terror from the spot, and they wouldn't have been able to sit now talking so calmly about what they had seen.'

'I'm a qualified nurse,' Karyn retorted with a thin smile. 'Perhaps my training has endowed me with a stronger stomach. But it was quite a shock, I can assure you.'

'I'm positive it was.' His fingers tightened around her hand. 'Karyn, I want you to know that I think you're a wonderful girl.'

'Thank you.' She smiled. 'I'm doing

my best. But life in these parts seems to be most eventful.'

'That I can promise you,' he said, smiling tensely. 'But it won't be as bad as it might have become had I not stood firm on my father's principles.'

'You're talking about the object of Marfissa's visit,' she said.

'That's right. So you overheard something of what was said!'

'Just a little. I was breathless when I reached the end of the *piazza* there. It was while I was recovering my breath that I overheard what was passing between you. It's none of my business, of course, but I think you're very wise, Paul.'

'Thank you.' His grip tightened still more, but he wasn't hurting her. 'I'm glad you see it the way I do.'

'Is it smuggling?' she asked. 'That's what it sounded like to me.'

'Smuggling!' He nodded slowly. 'It isn't a crime in the eyes of the islanders.'

'But that doesn't make it legal,' she pointed out.

They sat talking until a car drew up outside, and Paul went out to meet the visitor. Karyn steeled herself for the ordeal that was to come, and her heart thumped madly as Paul returned with several large men at his heels. The foremost of the newcomers was shorter than his companions, and he stepped forward with an air of authority about him. This would be the usurper inspector, Karyn thought, and Paul introduced him as Zoulas.

Inspector Zoulas was short in stature but wide in girth. He had a Grecian face that was almost classical, and Karyn found his personality strong and compelling. She couldn't take her eyes from his face as he sat down opposite her and began to ask questions. He spoke in English although Karyn assured him she was quite at ease speaking Greek.

He soon drew from her the salient facts of her discovery, and Paul supplied several lanterns to the waiting policeman. One of them carried a folded stretcher and another had several coils of rope slung across one broad shoulder.

'Now if you would accompany us, Miss Gregory,' Zoulas said, getting to his feet. 'I would like you to show us exactly where this body was lying when you discovered it.'

'I know the spot quite well, Inspector,' Paul said quickly. 'Miss Gregory has had quite a shock as it is. Surely you can spare her a return to the scene. The inlet is in front of my boathouse. I can find it in the dark with my eyes closed.'

'You may come along to assist,' Zoulas said quietly. 'But I need Miss Gregory along to identify the body.'

'But she wouldn't know who he is,' Paul protested sharply.

'I am aware of that. All I want to know is that the body we may recover is the one that she saw earlier.'

'I'm quite willing to go back down there,' Karyn said slowly. 'It doesn't matter, Paul.'

He nodded and came to help her to her feet. Two of the policemen preceded them along the path, and Paul took hold of Karyn's arm as they started the descent. She tremored with strange emotions at their contact, and some of the shock she was feeling was dissipated by his proximity. But she could not help wondering what was at the bottom of the brutal murder that had taken place, and the knowledge that she and Paul had probably heard it occurring filled her with tension. She was suddenly touched by a chill premonition as she watched the flickering lanterns held by the policemen ahead of them. She had arrived here on this beautiful Ionian island to help a crippled girl regain her health and happiness, but she had plunged into a far more serious situation, and she could not forget Paul's words of the previous evening when she had remarked upon the strange, grim noises they'd heard. The island had a darker side, and that side was stained with blood!

8

There was a nightmarish atmosphere at the inlet as the police recovered the body. Karyn stood with Paul at a distance and watched the grim operation. Paul moved in when the body was lying face upwards on the sand, and Karyn stifled a shudder as she watched. Zoulas knelt briefly on one knee, peering intently at the dead face, and Paul hovered over him before turning away and coming back to Karyn's side.

'Is it Michael's nephew?' she demanded breathlessly.

'Yes.' Paul's voice was harsh. 'Come along, there's no need for you to remain here any longer. Zoulas said I could take you back to the house.'

Karyn turned away eagerly, and her mind was throbbing with concern as they retraced their steps through the growing night. Paul walked easily, with the confidence of familiarity in his strides, and Karyn clung to his arm, fearful of the shadows, anxious and uncertain. They remained silent until they had negotiated the difficult cliff path, then Paul paused, and they stood staring down at the flickering lanterns that marked the spot where the police worked on the body.

'I'm sorry about all this, Karyn,' Paul said suddenly. 'I wish you hadn't suffered this experience. It won't put you off Sporveza, will it?'

'No. I shall stay. It was a bit unnerving, but I understand that these things do happen.' She heard him sigh, and she turned to him instinctively, feeling cold inside.

'Karyn, do you think we should take Nerissa away from the island?' he demanded. 'A change of scenery and atmosphere would be good medicine, wouldn't it?'

'Yes,' she agreed slowly. 'But would Nerissa go from here? Her trouble is that shock has bound her to that attic as securely as chains would. Perhaps it is a bit early to think in that direction, but we must bear it in mind.'

'So tomorrow we shall take her out with us, try to get her to start living again. And we must put on an act for her benefit, mustn't we?' He leaned towards her and Karyn caught her breath. 'It won't be difficult to play this game of romance,' he said huskily, and his arms slid around her shoulders and drew her into his strong embrace.

Karyn closed her eyes and let herself go. She needed something to combat the shock that gripped her, and Paul's demanding lips against her mouth aroused passion inside her, an emotion strong enough to fight off the paralysing effects of what she had discovered in the water.

For a long time they stood silent and motionless, their figures as one in the shadows. Then they heard the faint sounds of the policemen ascending the cliff path with their grim burden, and Paul sighed as he released Karyn reluctantly.

'Come, let us go into the house,' he said. 'I expect Zoulas will want to ask me some questions.'

'Why you?' Karyn demanded concernedly. 'What can you tell him?'

'Don't sound alarmed,' he replied confidently. 'I'm not mixed up in anything. I'm about the only man on this island who isn't, and the fact that Zoulas will talk to me proves that I'm clean.'

'But Marfissa was here this evening,' she went on hesitantly. 'I know it's none of my business, but he seems to be a strong personality.'

'He has a lot of influence on the island, but I am above him,' Paul said as they crossed the *piazza*. 'I have a large business to run, Karyn, and sidelines have no interest for me. My life is taken up with the business and with Nerissa. The only likely addition to that closed circle is you.'

'Me!' Karyn took a shuddering breath as she stared at his pale face. The light coming from the windows of the house gleamed reflectively in his eyes.

'I've been looking for a girl like you,' he commented, taking her arm and leading her into the house. 'I knew at a glance that you could become very important to me. But I don't want to frighten you off with such talk. No doubt you think we foreigners are very bold.'

'I don't look upon you as a foreigner!' she said firmly. 'I have foreign blood in my veins too, remember. I'm half English and half Greek, and I have a feeling that the Greek half of me is uppermost.'

'That's a great advantage.' He smiled as they entered the *salotto*. Miranda stood there, and Paul paused and studied the housekeeper's face for a moment. There was a look of enquiry on her dark features, and Karyn saw Paul nod slowly in response to the unspoken question. 'I'm sorry, Miranda,' he said gently. 'It is Ari. He's dead.'

Miranda nodded fatalistically and turned away, her lips compressed, her eyes bright with sharp emotion, and Karyn felt her heart go out to the woman. She looked up at Paul, almost angry at the situation that was permitted to reign here over the lovely island.

'Can nothing be done by the police to stop this dreadful night activity?' she demanded.

'That's your English half talking,' he replied with a slow smile. 'This isn't England, Karyn. Although it is sad about Ari, he knew the risks when he participated. No doubt he was actively engaged in smuggling, and his death is the result of some disagreement arising between him and his associates. As I've already told you, it is better for us to ignore what is going on. It doesn't concern me. I am not mixed up in it, so I am an outsider as much as you. I have to be careful, Karyn, or I might end up in the same way my parents did.'

'Your parents!' Karyn stared at him in surprise. 'But that was an accident, wasn't it?'

'Who knows?' His face was set in harsh lines, his eyes bright as he narrowed them. 'My father stood out against the islanders, and he experienced trouble because of it. Pressure has been brought against me.'

'Marfissa?' she demanded tensely.

'That's right.' He nodded. 'You heard my reply to his persuasion this evening, didn't you?'

'Yes. You turned his offer down flat.' Karyn was relieved as some of the puzzling pieces of the situation slipped into place. 'But why were you so afraid of that old gypsy we saw in Khalmia today?'

'Loukas Benassis! You noticed then!'

'I did. Can't you tell the police what you know, Paul, and hope that they can clean up the situation? Inspector Zoulas is an outsider. But he seems to be a very thorough man, and a good policeman. I'm sure he would welcome any assistance you can give him.'

'I have told him that very thing many times,' a sharp voice said from the doorway, and Karyn turned quickly to see Zoulas standing there, a grim expression upon his face. 'Perhaps the death of Ari Pouloura will add weight to my arguments. Ari was a close friend, Paul, was he not?'

'A very good friend,' Paul replied, his face stiff with tension.

'And you suspect that the deaths of your parents may not have been so accidental,' the inspector continued. 'I could have told you that a long time ago, but I didn't want to precipitate the case. May I come in?'

'Please do.' Paul shook himself from his shock. 'What do you know about my parents, Inspector? Or are you just trying to put the pressure on me. You know how serious this business is. Do you want me to finish up floating in the bay with a knife in my back?'

Karyn gasped, and Paul put a protective, reassuring hand upon her shoulder. They faced the policeman together, and he nodded slowly as he looked from one intent face to the other.

'It won't be easy for any of us,' he pointed out. 'I came here to Sporveza to do exactly what I've told you. I must break the stranglehold of these nocturnal activities. It could be tried with force, but naval craft in the bay and the straits would not nip the trouble in the bud, and that's where it has to be done. You could help me, Paul. I have offered you protection, and it would be thorough.'

'And if you succeeded, Inspector, you would go away,' Paul said. 'But the islanders would still be here, and they would not forget that I turned informer. I would be dead before your boat left the harbour.' He shook his head. 'You have no right to ask me to risk that.'

'I think Paul is right, Inspector,' Karyn said impulsively.

For a moment Zoulas stared at them. Then he nodded slowly, and bid them a goodnight. They both replied shortly and the policeman departed. When Zoulas had gone Paul sighed heavily. He still held Karyn by one shoulder, and she turned to him, wanting to be kissed again, but her desire was weighted by the knowledge that danger could attend Paul at any time. This whole thing was assuming a greater seriousness than she had dreamed was possible. Zoulas even suspected that the tragedy which had taken Paul's parents and almost killed Nerissa was not purely accidental, and Karyn was thoughtful as Paul took her into his arms.

'Karyn, I don't want anything to happen to you,' he said softly.

'Me!' She pulled back and stared into his intent face. 'Why should anything happen to me? Shouldn't I have reported discovering the body? Surely whoever killed Ari realized that sooner or later the body would be found.'

'It isn't that so much,' he said. 'They may think I will tell you all I know.'

'But that's absurd, Paul.'

'Nevertheless I should like you and Nerissa to go away from here for a short time. We have a villa on a smaller island not far away, and you would be safe there.'

'Will Nerissa agree to it? Paul, what

did Zoulas mean when he talked about the deaths of your parents? Wasn't it an accident? Do you know what really happened? Is there some other explanation? I'm beginning to think that Nerissa's trouble lies not in the knowledge that she failed her parents by making the wrong decision, but that something happened during the storm that was, to her mind, far worse and more shocking.'

'Perhaps you're right.' Paul's hands tightened upon her shoulders. 'And if I thought there was any truth in the supposition I would do everything in my power to help Zoulas and risk the consquences. But Nerissa has stuck to the story which you have heard, and I believe she is telling the truth. Zoulas is first a policeman, and I wouldn't put it past him to use some tale like that to try and put pressure on me.'

Karyn could not relax in his arms, and when Paul fetched her a drink she began to pace the room. He watched her with a half smile upon his rugged face.

'Come now,' he said at length. 'There's no need for you to worry so much. I'm sure Inspector Zoulas has everything under control, but he wouldn't admit it, would he?'

'I'm not sure,' Karyn replied. 'But where does that old gypsy come into it, Paul? You were scared of facing him in town today. The inspector interrupted when I asked you about him just now.'

'Loukas Benassis! He's an influential man, Karyn, and one with whom I want no dealings. He runs a more dangerous business than mere smuggling. He goes through the Iron Curtain when there is money to be made. I refused to let him use one of my ships as a rendezvous in the straits, and he lost a passenger because of it. I didn't know he was back on Sporveza when we saw him this afternoon. His presence here can only mean more trouble for the island.'

'Then why didn't you tell Inspector Zoulas about him?'

'You heard my reasons, Karyn. My life wouldn't be worth a pebble from the beach if I was foolish enough to tell what I know.'

'Wouldn't it be better for you to leave the island until the inspector has settled it all?' she demanded.

'I have thought of that, but no doubt the blame would be laid at my door if things started happening in my absence.' He shook his head. 'No, Karyn, I have to stay and face this out to the very end.'

They talked around the subject for some time, and then Paul insisted that she should go to bed. Karyn nodded sleepily and departed, leaving him to think by himself, and before going to her own room she went up to the attic to check that Nerissa was all right. The girl was sleeping peacefully in her bed, and for some moments Karyn stood staring down at the composed face, wondering what secrets lay in the girl's mind. What she had heard during the evening had set her thinking seriously, and she knew she had to find out more about the accident before she could best judge how to handle Nerissa.

When she finally went to bed she lay in the darkness trying to forget what she had seen on the beach. Finding a corpse was a shocking business, and on top of that there had been the revelations made of the true situation existing on Sporveza. She was shocked to the core, and her mind protested at the agony as she tried to sleep. When she did eventually sleep she lay mindless until the morning . . .

Next day Nerissa was not so well. She refused to go down to the bathroom, and lay with her face to the wall, stubbornly resisting Karyn's attempts at conversation. Karyn tried every trick in the book to recapture the girl's attention, but she might well have been talking to the wall itself for all the notice Nerissa took of her.

After doing what she could for the girl, Karyn realized that she was wasting her time, and probably making matters worse by her insistence, and she left the attic and went in search of

Paul. Her spirits sank when she learned from Miranda that Paul had left the house early and did not expect to return all day.

'I thought he was on holiday, Miranda,' Karyn said slowly.

'That's the way his holidays are,' the housekeeper replied.

Karyn nodded. She could understand now why Paul had no time for the lesser things in life, those things which made life worth living. She wandered out to the *piazza* to stare down at the sea, thinking all the time of Paul. There was a tiny knot of warm emotion trapped in the wider expanse of cold reasoning that filled her. She was afraid of many things now, indeterminate things that could not really be identified when analysed. So much was taking place behind the scenes on the island, under cover and secretly, and there seemed to be a sinister aspect that lay beneath the suface, hidden, yet plain to the discerning eye. It frightened Karyn, but she would not admit it to herself.

The day was long without Paul around, and each time that she tried to communicate with Nerissa, Karyn came up against blankness. In the evening she was so exasperated that she decided to try and shock the crippled girl out of her mood.

'Nerissa,' she said. 'Did you hear about the body I discovered on the beach?'

The girl looked at her, shock and surprise mingling in her dark eyes. She opened her mouth as if to speak, but thought better of it and remained silent. She turned her gaze away from Karyn.

'Tell me what really happened in the accident when your parents were drowned, Nerissa!' Karyn met the girl's glance with determined eyes. 'You told everyone that it was an accident, but I think your mental condition stems from something even more shocking than the story you gave. What happened? Who was on that yacht with you, apart from your parents.'

'No-one!' At last Nerissa found her tongue. Karyn felt a flicker of triumph. She had succeeded in breaking the girl's impassiveness. 'Why don't you leave me alone, Karyn? Is this the way a nurse is supposed to help me?'

'I'm doing my best but you won't co-operate. You don't want to get well, Nerissa, and shall I tell you why?' She paused, wanting the girl's attention.

'If you think you have worked out a theory then I shall be glad to hear it,' Nerissa retorted obstinately.

'I think you're afraid to go out because someone may be waiting to finish off what he started that day on the yacht.'

'No!' The girl's voice sounded like a strangled gasp. Her harsh expression vanished and fear took its place, twisting her beautiful lips and filling her eyes with pain. 'How can you think that? It is absurd! I told the truth, and that was painful enough. I had to admit that I made a mistake.'

'Which was easier than admitting that someone in the background had planned the whole thing,' Karyn added. 'Your parents didn't die as the result of an accident, Nerissa. Someone wanted your father dead and you could do nothing to stop him. Yet you dare not tell of what you know. This is the reason for your paralysis! You have strong feelings of guilt, and they are locked away in your subconscious mind. You wouldn't be like this if you only thought you had failed your parents, because you did the best you could for them in that yacht. Your conscience was satisfied with your attempts. But my theory is more in keeping with the medical facts about your type of mental illness. Now tell me that I am wrong, Nerissa. Lie to me here and now, if you can. Picture your parents, and tell me that they died accidently, when you know they are not resting easily in their graves. Is that the reason why you keep yourself imprisoned in this attic? Are you afraid that their restless spirits will find you in those other rooms where once they were alive and happy?'

The girl covered her eyes with her hands and began to sob. Karyn felt sympathy for her, but did not show her true feelings. Paul was in some kind of danger if those mysterious men suspected he was informing the police. But there was another way the inspector could get at the root of the situation, and that was through Nerissa. Karyn knew she could not slacken her efforts.

'Do you know that Paul is in danger of losing his life?' she continued. 'You saw your parents die, and perhaps it was intended that you should die with them, but you were spared, Nerissa, and probably because you can put the blame where it rightly belongs. Have you thought of that? You might be the instrument of vengeance. But you skulk up here, crippled more in your mind than body, and you make no effort to see that the deaths of your parents are avenged. I thought the spirit of revenge ran strongly through the Greeks. I am half Greek myself, and I know what I would do were I in your position.'

'It isn't as easy as that,' Nerissa said brokenly, her shoulders shaking as she cried. 'You just don't understand, Karyn.'

'Try and make me,' Karyn insisted. 'I'll tell you something, Nerissa. If you wanted, you could get off that bed now and walk like any normal girl. There's nothing physically wrong with you. Your mind, your feelings of guilt are binding you to that bed. Don't you sometimes feel the urge to walk again, Nerissa?'

'You are cruel!' the girl said brokenly. Her sobbing continued unabated, and Karyn caught her breath and shook her head slowly as she resisted the impulse to go on and on in an attempt to break this girl's hold upon her own mind.

'I'm sorry, Nerissa,' she said slowly. 'But can't you see that I have to be cruel to be kind to you? This is a fight we have on our hands, and unless we do fight then you will never get up on your feet and walk. The longer this battle is put off the more difficult it will be.'

'I don't want to hear any more tonight,' the girl said desperately. 'Please leave me alone, Karyn.'

Karyn nodded and left the room. She went down to the *piazza* to stand staring at the darkly concealed sea. The shadows were thick because the moon had not yet arisen, and she shivered as she relived the shock of the previous evening. She wished Paul would return, and started nervously when a voice spoke to her out of the darkness of the corner near the garden.

'I hope I'm not disturbing you, but I have taken advantage of the fact that Paul is not here to come and have a talk with you.'

Karyn caught her breath as the shadows moved and a tall figure appeared before her.

'Good evening, Mr Marfissa,' she replied in fairly even tones. 'Does anyone know you're here?'

'No. I wanted to be unannounced,' he retorted, and Karyn saw that he was holding a glass in his hand. 'I have the liberty of making myself at home here whenever I want. Would you care to walk with me into the garden? There is a summer house where we can talk undisturbed.'

'What is it you have to say to me?' she demanded.

'Any man would want to talk to you,' he countered. 'Paul is fortunate in having secured so beautiful a nurse for his sister. But I wish to talk to you in private, and I don't like to be interrupted. Miranda will be through to light the lanterns at any time now, and I would rather she didn't know I was here.'

'Very commendable!' Karyn smiled thinly. 'Is it because you are suspected of knowing something about the death of her husband's nephew?'

'You have picked up quite a lot in your short time here.' He was severe, and Karyn could not help feeling a twinge of alarm. 'The reason I came this evening is because last evening I detected a sort of sympathy in you for Paul. I'm a very sensitive man and I can see these things. No doubt that sympathy will turn into love before very long, but that is of no concern to me. I want to use your sympathy for Paul. If you can make him see sense then you will have a man to love, but if nothing can change his mind and his opinions then I'm afraid I shall lose a very good friend.'

'You're threatening me with a threat against Paul's life,' Karyn said thinly. 'I'm afraid I have no influence with him.'

'Then you'd better try and get some!' There was a harshness in the back of his voice, and Karyn shivered to hear it. 'If he cannot be dissuaded from certain objects he has decided upon then tragedy will strike again at the Stephan family. This is no threat. I am a friend of Paul's and I am concerned about him, I would be greatly upset if anything should happen to him. If you do have any feelings about him then do something before it is too late.'

Karyn remained silent, and he came closer to peer into her face. She watched him intently, seeing the faint gleam of his eyes and teeth, but it was too dark for either of them to see the other's expression.

'I think you should talk to Paul again

if you are that much of a friend to him,' Karen said finally, and he made an impatient sound and turned away.

'I have done all I can in that direction,' he retorted. 'I have even taken a great risk by coming here to try and enlist your aid in this. But I can do no more. You may tell Paul of my visit this evening if you wish, but now I must go. Goodnight, Miss Gregory.'

'Goodnight, Mr Marfissa.' Karyn relaxed as his dark figure crossed the *piazza* and disappeared from her sight. She set her teeth into her bottom lip and worried herself with the thoughts of what might happen, and she didn't even hear Miranda come out to light the lanterns. When the housekeeper appeared, Karyn started nervously.

'I am sorry, Karyn Miranda said quickly. 'I thought you had gone to bed. I thought I heard voices out here a short time ago and imagined it was Paul who had returned.'

'I haven't seen him, Miranda. Have you any idea when he will be back?'

'I cannot say. He has some very important business to take care of. Is anything wrong? You sound a little upset.'

'It's nothing really.' Karyn shook her head, aware that Miranda was watching her closely. 'I've had a set to with Nerissa in an attempt to get her to make some progress, but it didn't go as well as I hoped and I'm upset about it.'

'You mustn't let it become too personal,' Miranda said wisely. 'You have to tell yourself that it is for the good of the patient, and do what you think is right.'

'That's all I have to guide me,' Karyn told her.

'You're making her think for herself, and that's a good start. Don't despair, Karyn. I do know how it makes you feel because I have had quite a lot of it with Nerissa. But I'm sure you will do the right thing, and then all will be well.'

Karyn nodded, trying to believe Miranda's words, although she knew them to be true. The housekeeper pattered away, and Karyn began pacing the *piazza*. She was lost in thought until she heard a car coming, and then she knew Paul was home and immediately felt easier. She was seated at the table when he came on to the *piazza*.

'Karyn!' He came forward quickly and she arose to her feet to greet him. 'I am sorry you've been left alone all day, but it was unavoidable. However I shall be able to relax tomorrow, and we'll take Nerissa out with us, shall we? Has everything been all right here today?'

'The same as usual,' she reported gently, and as she faced him he took her into his arms.

'I've missed you,' he said as he kissed her. 'I haven't been able to concentrate at all because of you.'

Karyn was thrilled by his words, but in the back of her mind was the knowledge induced by Lanni Marfissa' words, and she was afraid as she tried to relax with this handsome man who was becoming increasingly important to her.

9

The next day was the most important one yet, Karyn decided soon after she had made her first appearance in Nerissa's room. The girl seemed subdued after their conversation of the evening before, and Karyn was surprised when Nerissa agreed to take a drive with Paul.

'I have to make the effort,' she said slowly, her dark eyes searching Karyn's face. 'You will be there, and I think you can give me the strength I shall need. But I want to see Paul in different surroundings, to try and judge what he is feeling. You succeeded in making me think last night, Karyn, and I thank you for it.'

'Then my presence here is justified,' Karyn replied with a smile. 'Don't worry about anything, Nerissa. I'm sure it will all come right in the end.'

She went down to seek out Paul, and was relieved when he appeared and told her that they had the day free. When she told him about Nerissa his eyes shone.

'Thats' wonderful news. Let's go away before she changes her mind. I'll put the wheelchair in the boot, and if we stop anywhere we can take her with us. But do you think she will be all right, Karyn?'

'I think so. We have to take this chance to find out.'

After breakfast Karyn went to prepare Nerissa for the trip, and found the girl excited and nervous. She tried to calm her with conversation, but by the time Paul arrived to carry his sister down to the car Nerissa was in a state of nerves. Miranda preceded them out to the car with the large hamper packed with food. Nerissa cried out when the sunlight struck her eyes, and Karyn hastened to Paul's side to take the girl's hand, afraid that another outburst was coming, but Nerissa had set her teeth into her lip, and she was silent as Paul placed her in the back seat of the car and stepped back to study her anxiously.

Karyn got into the back with the girl, and sat holding her hands. Miranda handed over a pair of sun glasses, and Nerissa seemed to relax when the sun was shut off from her dark eyes. Paul wasted no time in driving away, and when Karyn glanced back she saw Miranda waving hopefully. She replied to the housekeeper's farewell, and turned to start occupying Nerissa's mind, knowing that the first few minutes were the most exacting for the girl.

After a time Karyn began to talk, and Nerissa answered, hesitantly at first but showing more interest as the miles slipped by. Paul did not stop at any time during the morning, and avoided the town and the village. They met little in the way of traffic on the road, and by the time Karyn suggested they stop for lunch she was reasonably certain that Nerissa had overcome the first and most difficult hurdle.

Paul stopped the car in a gateway, and beyond it the ground stretched away, wild and beautiful, to the mountains inland. As he got out of the car he pointed up the hill to a spot near the top where the grass was thick and comfortable, and Karyn agreed it was an ideal spot for a picnic. She carried the hamper while Paul gathered Nerissa in his arms and started up the steep slope. By the time they reached the spot he had chosen he was breathless and hot.

'I am sorry, Paul,' Nerissa said as he eased her down on to the blanket Karyn had brought along.

'Nonsense,' he retorted lightly. 'This is the happiest day I have known for a very long time, Nerissa. I hope you will continue to make progress. Very soon you will be running around here on your own two feet.'

Karyn saw the harshness which flooded Nerissa's face, and she hurriedly intervened.

'What a beautiful scene from here,'

she said joyfully. 'You can see the sea in the distance. What a glorious shade of blue!'

'It's wonderful,' Paul enthused. 'I have been here several times, but today it seems all the better for having Nerissa along. This is better than being cooped up in the attic, isn't it, Nerissa?'

'Yes,' the girl said in doubtful, hesitant tones, and Karyn flashed Paul a warning glance as she unfastened the hamper.

'Would you like to help with the food, Nerissa?' she demanded. 'You're going to find the need to start doing things again.'

'Do you think it will be any use?' Nerissa demanded. 'I think you both are fooling yourselves. I shall never be able to walk.'

'If you think like that then I'll have to agree with you,' Paul said sharply, and once again Karyn tried to lead the talk into safer channels.

They ate, and afterwards Nerissa settled down to have a nap. Karyn made the girl comfortable, and then helped Paul repack the hamper. She went with him back down to the car, and in the shelter of a tree by the roadside he took her into his arms. Karyn had never felt happier as he kissed her. But she dared not let her attention wander from Nerissa, and from time to time her eyes lifted to the spot where the girl lay.

'You're a very good nurse, Karyn,' Paul told her, holding her tightly in his embrace. 'I shall be eternally grateful for what you have done for my sister. Poor little Nerissa! But this time last week there was no hope for her. I had visions of sending her off to a hospital, and once she had entered it she would never have come out again.'

Karyn nodded, happy, vibrant with wonderful emotion. She was too full for words. Her patient was making unexpected progress, and on top of that her own feelings for this handsome man were getting out of control, swelling with hope and anticipation. Karyn had never been in love before, and the pangs of this strange awakening in her breast were both keen and overwhelming. Marfissa had said he noticed sympathy in her for Paul. But it hadn't been sympathy, she was certain. Marfissa had seen the birth of love, and had been unable to recognize it as such.

They stayed together for a timeless period, and nothing disturbed them. There was very little traffic on the road, and the peacefulness that attended the spot seemed charged with enchantment. Paul was content to be with Karyn, and she sensed his growing ease. Her presence was helping both brother and sister. But beyond that a whole new horizon stretched out before her, exciting and strange, promising much and luring her on with a whole range of wonderful new emotions. She was like a schoolgirl standing on the threshold of fairyland. She had to go on, despite the warnings of Marfissa and the situation that surrounded the death of Ari Pouloura. She felt that she had been brought to this island by an obscure chance, and her arrival here had been awaited by both brother and sister. Now she was here and destiny had to be fulfilled. But what was her destiny? Had she been brought here for the sole purpose of helping these two needy people, or was her future entwined with theirs?

A call from the hillside sent Karyn hurrying upwards, and Paul raced at her side. When they reached the spot where they had left Nerissa they found the girl awake and peering around. Karyn anxiously scanned Nerissa's face, and was reassured by the expression she saw.

'I've been asleep, Karyn,' the girl cried in wonder, and Paul laughed excitedly at the normal note in his sister's tones.

'How do you feel?' Karyn demanded, seating herself by the girl and taking her hand.

'Wonderful! That's the only word to describe it.' Nerissa turned to her and hugged her impulsively. 'I can feel the good you are doing me, Karyn. Shall I soon be able to walk, do you think?'

'We'll get started on some exercises

now,' Karyn replied. 'It will take time, but if you maintain this frame of mind then the possibilities are enormous.'

'Let's go on,' Nerissa suggested. 'I want to drive all day, Paul, and see all the places I've been hiding from. 'The ghosts are still there, but today they haven't any fears for me. Don't let us waste a minute of my feelings. Tomorrow I may be back where I was yesterday.'

'Don't even think like that,' Karyn ordered as Paul lifted his sister. 'We're on a straight track now and there's no time for you to look back. Keep reaching upwards, Nerissa, and all will be well.'

The rest of the day passed quickly, and by the time they returned to the house Nerissa was utterly exhausted, but happy. Karyn noted the gleam in the girl's eyes as Paul carried her indoors, and when they met Miranda in the hall she placed a hand on Paul's arm.

'Just a moment, Paul,' she said firmly. 'I told Miranda this morning to strip the attic. Nerissa isn't going back up there. Her old room is ready for her and that's where she's going now.'

There was a silence after her words that seemed charged with electricity. Paul stared at Karyn with a startled expression in his eyes, but it was Nerissa she was watching, and she saw the girl's lips compress. For a moment she thought she had overdone it, but then the girl smiled.

'Karyn,' she said in surprise. 'You certainly know your job. For the past hour I've been feeling dread at the thought of returning here, and I was beginning to think it was the house itself. But it's not the house. It's the thought of returning to the attic that's hurting me, although I didn't realize it until you spoke. That attic is all that you say. It has an atmosphere that's stained with the gloom and the misery of the past. I don't want to go up there. Take me to my old room, Paul, and I'll prove to you that I have made progress today.'

'Nerissa!' He was almost overcome

with happiness, and Karyn smiled as he kissed the girl passionately, his relief knowing no bounds. He started up the stairs with the slight figure resting happily in his arms, and Nerissa stared at Karyn with new happiness smiling from her face.

Miranda took hold of Karyn's arm as she followed, and for a moment the happiness which the woman was feeling for Nerissa was clouded by anxiety as she whispered in Karyn's ear.

'Marfissa says he must talk with you, Karyn. I don't know what this is all about, but Paul must not know this man has seen you.'

'I'll come and talk to you when Nerissa is settled in her room,' Karyn said hurriedly, and the housekeeper nodded and went back to her kitchen. Karyn went on up the stairs, and her relief at the way Nerissa settled into her old room was overshadowed by the strange fear which had invaded her mind at the housekeeper's words. Trouble was perching like a vulture on a high rock, peering down at the scene with knowing eyes, and Karyn wondered what had happened during the day to force Lanni Marfissa into approaching Miranda. Was the trouble in the background beginning to loom larger? Was the balance of good and evil changing? Nerissa was making progress, but on the other hand Paul seemed to be slipping deeper into danger. Karyn could sense it, and her strange emotions, which seemed to proclaim love for her patient's brother, filled her with urgent fears. It seemed to her that Nerissa herself held the key to the puzzle, but the girl had more than enough to cope with for herself without the added burden of her brother's danger to retard her.

When they left the girl in her room Paul took Karyn's hands in his own and squeezed them joyously. Then he drew her into his embrace, and she returned his ardour with eagerness. The progress which Nerissa was making filled Karyn with hopeful joy, and she could not prevent her hopes from overwhelming her fears. As they went down the stairs she was confidently happy for the first time in many hours.

She ate the evening meal with Paul on the *piazza*, and the intimacy of their solitude further strengthened the growing feelings that abounded inside her. Here was a man she had already come to regard highly in the very few short days of their acquaintance. Something inside her warned that he was going to prove more than an employer. Her surprise at discovering emotions for him in her mind was further deepened by her eagerness to get to know him better. Men had never entered into her calculations at any time, although there had been many eligible men in her life. Now she was knowing for the first time the nagging points of desire, the indecision that accompanied the enlarging awareness that here was a man who intrigued and attracted her.

The fact that he was attracted to her added to the power that seemed to surround them, and Karyn had the unusual feeling that all this had been planned for her long ago, before she was born. It was romantic to lay the improving situation at the feet of Fate or Destiny, but that was what she was doing, and despite the growing fears that danger threatened, she could not help believing that all would turn out well.

Even Nerissa's progress pointed to the wellbeing of their cause, and the dark thoughts of Lanni Marfissa in Karyn's mind seemed to lose their reality as she believed only what she wanted to.

When she took her leave of Paul to go to bed, Karyn had forgotten about Marfissa, but as she entered her room Miranda appeared behind her, cautioning silence with a trembling finger placed against her tight lips, and Karyn breathed deeply as tension entered her mind.

'I have been waiting for the chance to talk to you,' the housekeeper said. 'I have a message for you from Marfissa.'

'I'm sorry, Miranda, but I haven't

had the chance to slip away from Paul. He must know nothing about this.'

'I certainly agree with that,' Miranda retorted quickly. 'Paul would kill Marfissa if he knew about this.'

'You are loyal to Paul, so why are you helping Marfissa?'

'I am not helping him,' the woman said sharply. 'I am trying to protect Paul.'

'What does Marfissa want?'

'You, I expect.' Miranda was expressionless. 'He's a bad man, Karyn, and once he sets his mind upon something he won't give up easily. He has Paul's life in his hands, and no doubt he intends using Paul as a lever against you.'

'Why me?' Karyn was conscious of growing fear as she faced the woman. 'How is it that men like Marfissa can do as they please without fear of arrest, Miranda?'

'Because there are so few men like Paul on this island,' came the fierce reply. 'You know that Inspector Zoulas wants Paul to tell what he knows about Marfissa's organization, but Paul is not that kind of a fool. He would not live long enough to enjoy the freedom that the imprisonment of Marfissa and his kind would bring to the island.'

'If you care so much for Paul why don't you do something against Marfissa?'

'Because of my husband, Karyn. He has to work with Marfissa, the same as most of the island men. Why do you suppose Michael's nephew Ari was killed?'

'I don't know.' Karyn found it difficult to speak at all.

'Because he was a friend of Paul's, and had been heard to say on occasion that he would talk if Paul did.'

'What is this message you bring to me?' Karyn demanded.

'Marfissa wants to see you. He will be waiting by the cliff path tonight when everyone here is asleep.'

'Do you advise me to go and see him?' Karyn was cold inside at the thought of sneaking out of the house in the moonlight and meeting that tall, unpredictable Greek. She has sensed that Marfissa was not afraid of anything. He would carry out any threat he made, and she shivered as she thought of the dead Ari lying in the water with a knife in his back.

'I dare have no say in this,' Miranda said. 'I suppose it would be wiser for you to leave this place and return to England. Could you forget us now?'

'I've only been here a few days,' Karyn replied quickly. 'I couldn't walk out.'

'Then you have become involved with us, and you will take your place in this business even against your will. I'm not a superstitious woman, but I read the signs the moment you arrived. It is a great pity that this trouble had to be growing up around us. It was bad enough that Nerissa was crippled because of it.'

'That accident which killed her parents was not an accident at all, was it?' Karyn said stiffly. 'Nerissa as much as admitted that to me last night.'

'You are learning too much for your own good, Karyn. Don't make the mistake Nerissa did. She wanted to help her parents, and would have done if her father hadn't been struck down that afternoon on the yacht.'

'I thought he had a heart attack!'

'He did, but it was induced by pressures exerted against him. No-one knows exactly what happened, but it is certain that Marfissa was behind it.'

'Does Paul know this?'

'I doubt it or he would have done something about it before now.'

'When will Marfissa be on that path?' Karyn could feel a great nervousness growing inside her. 'Perhaps some plain talking will put him in his place.'

'You are not in England now,' Miranda said. 'Don't make the mistake of thinking that you will be able to handle Marfissa that easily.'

'I'm not thinking of myself,' Karyn pointed out. 'I must try to do something. If everyone else has his hands hands tied then I shall do what I can. I don't care about myself.'

'If some of our men had your courage this situation wouldn't have arisen.' There was a bitter note in Miranda's voice. 'Now I must go. It is my job to make sure the house is locked. I shall leave the kitchen door unbolted so that you may go out and come in without disturbing anyone. Push home the bolt when you return, and then no-one will be the wiser.'

Karyn nodded, already overcome by nervousness. She was stout hearted, but she didn't relish the thought of sneaking out of the house to meet a strange man whom she knew to be capable of anything up to murder. But there was Paul to consider, and if seeing Marfissa would help him then she was prepared to do what she could. She closed her door and sat upon the bed in darkness, waiting for the sounds of Paul going to his room. The moonlight was brighter now, and she crossed to the window to peer out at the smooth sea. It crossed her mind that she could not understand how this same sea could sweep up into such a violent storm that Nerissa's parents were drowned. Had

Nature conspired with Marfissa on that dreadful day? Marfissa could hardly have known that the yacht was going to be used on that particular day — unless — Karyn froze as the thought crossed her mind — unless Nerissa herself had arranged for the boat trip! Miranda had said the girl dared her father to go out in the growing storm. What had been the reason behind that?

She heard footsteps in the corridor, and went close to her door to listen. It had to be Paul going to bed, she thought grimly, still shaken by the foul notion which had crossed her mind. But why else would Nerissa have felt such a deep sense of guilt? Had the girl been acting on Marfissa's orders that day, unaware of what he really planned? Had the storm come as an additional aid to the man's grim plan? Had Nerissa guessed at the truth afterwards? Karyn tried to dislodge the train of thought from her mind. She listened intently, satisfying herself that the house was at last at rest.

The sound of her heartbeats seemed to echo across the dim corridor as she let herself out of her room, and Karyn had to clench her hands to control her wavering determination as she crept to the stairs and descended. She went through to the kitchen, and there paused when she stared out into the garden lying ghostly in the silvery moonlight. By thinking of Paul she was able to induce herself to go on, and she opened the door silently and went out into the keen air. Nervousness was like a caged bird in her breast and throat.

She went through the garden and gained the cliff path, peering around intently as she walked slowly along the top of the steep cliff. The moon sailed free in a wide and starry sky, but the shadows from the surrounding trees were thick and black, deceptive and frightening. Karyn walked on, filled with a dread of the unexpected, sensing that she was under observation already from Marfissa's deadly brown eyes. She was expecting him to confront her at any moment, but when a figure appeared from the shadows on her left it was all she could do to prevent a cry of shock from escaping past her compressed lips.

'You are a brave girl!' Marfissa spoke gently in little more than a whisper. 'I had begun to think that you would not come.'

'What is it you want with me?' Karyn demanded. 'If I am missed from the house there will be trouble.'

'How would you be missed?' he demanded. 'Is your room not private?'

'You know what I mean,' Karyn said in flat tones. Some of her fears had left her now he was in front of her. 'Just tell me what you want so that I can hurry and return to the house.'

'Your presence here proves to me just how much Paul means to you,' he said. 'That is all I wanted to know. It gives me power over you, Miss Gregory.'

'Haven't you enough power on this island without having to dominate every newcomer?' she countered sharply.

'Someone has been talking to you,

telling you things it would have been better you didn't know,' he retorted. 'I have little doubt who it is, and I shall have to reprove her. But to get back to the reason why I asked you out here tonight. I have heard that Paul is considering turning informer. That Inspector Zoulas is a very persuasive man. If you feel as keenly about Paul as I think you do you'll try to encourage him to leave the island. I have already asked you to do what you can to induce him to avoid being a menace. However the time is past for considerations. Although I love him as a brother I will not hesitate to have him removed. You are his only hope. I am reluctant to see him die, so if you can possibly get him away then do so. Use his sister as an excuse, but get him off the island and keep him away for several months. Will you do it?'

'How can I refuse to help save his life?' Karyn retorted. 'But how do I know that you are telling me the truth?'

'You will have to trust me. There is too much at stake for you to do anything but that. Paul will surely meet a bad end if he doesn't leave now. Do you understand that?'

'Yes,' Karyn said slowly, and she turned away from him, wishing to bring the meeting to an end. She kept well away from the edge of the cliff as she retraced her steps to the house, and it was all she could do to resist the impulse to turn and look back at him. Not until she reached the sanctury of her room did she relax, and only then could she begin to understand the deadly seriousness of what Marfissa had said.

Karyn got slowly into bed, her mind over-busy. It should be easy enough for her to get Nerissa away, but would Paul go along if the girl insisted? Karyn hoped so, and resolved to get Nerissa to put pressure on her brother. That should work, and only too well did she know the alternative if it didn't. Karyn realized that Marfissa had been serious in what he said. But there was a chance that everything would work out well, and she had to do whatever was necessary to bring it about. That much was clear to her as she drifted into sleep. In the morning she would act upon Marfissa's advice, even though she didn't trust the man . . .

10

Nerissa seemed a different girl the next morning, and Karyn was overjoyed that the progress she had made was maintained. The alarm that she felt about her talk with Marfissa seemed unreal in the bright morning sunlight, but she knew she must not underestimate the situation. Paul was in danger, and every step to prevent another tragedy in the Stephan family had to be taken.

'Now that you're feeling so much better I think it would be a good idea if you took a trip away from this island,' Karyn suggested after Nerissa had eaten her breakfast. 'Paul is on holiday, and he suggested that you might like to get away from it all.'

'Would he go with us?' the girl queried.

'I don't see why not!' Karyn's heart

lurched as she saw the chance she wanted. 'He's on holiday, isn't he?'

'But he doesn't like leaving the island,' Nerissa said.

'He would do anything to please you, Nerissa, and I think it would be better for his health if he left.'

'You think he's not well?' Concern showed in the girl's face.

'He's been under strain for a long time,' Karyn suggested.

'But that isn't what you're worried about. I can't forget what you said to me about my parents.'

Karyn sat down upon the bed and stared into the girl's face. Nerissa was staring across the room, her eyes filled with a faraway expression. The silence that enveloped them was tense and heavy.

'What really happened, Nerissa?' Karyn asked quietly. 'I think it's about time you told the truth. Paul's life is in danger. I didn't want to tell you this, but if there's anything you can do to help then you must do it regardless.

Lanni Marfissa has been around here several times in the past two days, and last night he talked to me. There's going to be bad trouble for Paul unless we can do something to stop it.'

'Has Marfissa threatened Paul's life?' Nerissa demanded.

'He warned me that something may happen to Paul, and suggested that I try and get him to leave the island for a time.'

'And you want me to get him away.' Nerissa nodded slowly. 'We must make the effort, Karyn. I should die if anything happened to Paul.'

'Inspector Zoulas would know what to do if evidence was given to him.' Karyn watched Nerissa's face for expression, hoping to gauge the girl's mood, but Nerissa looked blankly at her, and Karyn sighed heavily. 'You love your brother, don't you, Nerissa?' she demanded. 'But then you loved your parents, and it seems to me that you persuaded your father to go out in the yacht that day despite the storm. It's a harsh thing to say, but it looks as if you really caused your parents to die.'

'Why do you think I'm suffering like this?' the girl demanded bitterly. 'And why do you suppose I've kept quiet all these months? The same threats were made against me before the accident, but I swear that I didn't know what was going to happen on the yacht.

'I was told to get Father out of the way for the afternoon. It seemed a small thing to do at the time, and I was told that such an action would save us all a lot of trouble. You may not be able to understand this, Karyn, because you're a stranger among us and not acquainted with our ways. Lanni Marfissa has more power on the island than the police.'

'Only because no-one among the islanders will help the police,' Karyn retorted. 'But tell me what happened, Nerissa. What did Marfissa say to you on that day of the accident?'

'He told me that Father's life was in danger, just as he's saying it about Paul now. He told me he could put matters right if he was able to check through Father's papers here in the house, and that meant getting Father out of the way for the afternoon. He suggested that I get Father to take us out into the straits in the yacht, and that's what I did. I wanted to save my Father! Perhaps Lanni spoke the truth that day, I don't know. Perhaps he only wanted to look through the house as he'd said. But none of us knew that Father had been suffering heart trouble for years, and the strain when the storm broke was too much for him. He collapsed, and Mother nursed him in the cabin. I had to bring back the yacht alone!'

The girl broke off and buried her face in her hands. Karyn patted her shoulder gently. But Nerissa wasn't crying. She looked up at Karyn with a bright expression in her dark eyes.

'The yacht began to take water before we got back,' she said. 'With Father fit enough to handle her she would have made it all right, but he was stricken, and twice his heart stopped beating. Mother was keeping him alive by every bit of knowledge she had. That was why I took the risk of trying to get to the beach in the bay below here, but the yacht was too sluggish with the water she'd taken aboard, and we hit the rocks.'

Nerissa was stiff with dread as she relived those terrible moments, and Karyn took hold of the girl's hands and gripped them tightly. She didn't know if the effort to make this revelation would have an adverse effect upon Nerissa, but she had to get at the truth for Paul's sake. Nerissa's mental state was not as important as Paul's life, and now the girl herself knew it.

'You think that Marfissa knew there was something wrong with the yacht when you took it out?' Karyn demanded.

'No! I could never make up my mind to that. He came and saw me after I had recovered, and threatened again to make me keep quiet about it all. He said he had removed the threat from my father's life, from the family, too, although only Paul and I were left. It was too late for my parents.'

'Now Marfissa is threatening Paul's life,' Karyn said, sighing deeply. 'What can we do, Nerissa?'

'Get him away from the island,' came the swift retort. 'We can do that easily enough.'

'But wouldn't it be better for you to tell Inspector Zoulas about all this? If he could find something to pin on Marfissa perhaps all this trouble will come to an end. Don't you think Marfissa has been controlling the island long enough?'

'He has too many people in his power. Fear secures their loyalty. Even Miranda and Michael are working for him.'

'Miranda!' Karyn stared at the girl with disbelief in her blue eyes.

'How do you suppose Marfissa got into the house that afternoon we went out in the yacht?' Nerissa demanded.

'But Miranda is devoted to you!'

'And very afraid of Marfissa.' Nerissa

sighed heavily. 'I don't have to point out to you that Michael's nephew died because he failed to remain cowed. Ari was in love with me before the accident happened, and I used to torment him about his feelings. But he knew what really happened, and when he lined himself up with Paul against Marfissa I knew he would have to die. Your words came as no surprise when you told me about him.'

'And you will do nothing to try and put a stop to Marfissa?' Karyn demanded.

'What can I do that will help?' The girl shrugged. 'If I telephoned for Zoulas to come and see me Marfissa would know about it before the inspector. Whom do you think would get here first?'

'And you're prepared to stay here in your room and wait for Paul to die?'

'There is nothing I can do.' Nerissa spoke listlessly. 'I am a cripple and of little consequence. Even if we got Paul away from the island something would happen to him. Perhaps that is what Marfissa wants. Have you thought of that? He may want Paul away from here because to kill him on the island may be too dangerous.'

Karyn thought that over, and shook her head. She didn't find the situation any clearer because of what Nerissa had told her. She sighed heavily as she got to her feet.

'What are you going to do, Karyn?' the girl demanded. 'I hope you won't be rash and precipitate trouble.'

'I'm going to ask Paul to take us out again today,' Karyn replied, forcing a smile. 'Now that we've got your feet on the road to recovery we have to chase you along it.'

Leaving the room, she paused on the stairs and allowed her mind to consider what she had learned. But there was not enough evidence for the Inspector to work on. He would need certain proof of Marfissa's guilt before being able to act. Miranda came to the foot of the stairs, and the housekeeper's face was showing anxiety as she looked up at the motionless Karyn.

'You are worried about something, Karyn,' the housekeeper observed. 'Was it last night?'

Karyn studied the woman's tense face, and realized that Miranda was very much afraid. The fact that the housekeeper had left the kitchen door unbolted for her last night proved just how deeply Miranda was in Marfissa's clutches, and she guessed it would be true of all the other islanders. There would be no help forthcoming from these people. Karyn went slowly down the stairs to confront Miranda.

'I received a warning last night,' she said urgently. 'Paul must leave the island or else. Do you think there is any danger to him?'

'If Marfissa told you that then believe him,' Miranda said quickly, her face paling.

'How loyal are you, Miranda?' Karyn demanded.

'More than you know, or think,' came the swift reply. 'I can guess what you are thinking, but I have my husband to consider. Don't forget that, Karyn.'

'So that's where your pressure point lies,' Karyn said, nodding. 'And no doubt they keep your husband in line by using you.'

'That is the way of it,' the woman agreed. 'They have a chain of silence on the island, and each link is a human being under sentence of death. That is the way Marfissa works.'

'Then it is no use appealing to you for help,' Karyn mused. 'Very well, Miranda. I do understand, and I sympathize with you.'

A door slammed, and Karyn looked around to see Paul coming towards them. He smiled, and she thought of him lying dead in the place of the man she had discovered in the water. She shivered because her imagination made it seem so real. But she forced an answering smile as he paused before them.

'What are we doing today?' he demanded. 'How is Nerissa, Karyn?'

'Fine, and wanting to go out. If we

keep this up all week then surely she will be well on the way to recovering completely.'

'But what about her legs?' he demanded. 'She won't be back to normal until she can walk.'

'That may come later,' Karyn said slowly. 'Don't count on anything, Paul, but once her mind is straightened out her nerves will get a chance to relax.'

'I'm waiting for that day,' he replied. 'Miranda, get that hamper ready again. We're going out for the day. Do you think Karyn is ready to go aboard the yacht again, Karyn?'

'The yacht!' She stared at him tensely, shaking her head doubtfully. 'I don't know, Paul. It might put her right back to the start again. She had some fearsome experiences on that vessel. Perhaps it is a bit early yet.'

'All right. We do want her to walk before she runs. I'll try and keep patient. But it's been so long since she walked around!'

Karyn nodded. She understood how

he felt. But she knew that he was not aware of his own danger, and she took hold of his arm as Miranda went towards the kitchen.

'I must talk to you, Paul,' she said.

'Certainly.' He stared at her, then turned back to his study. 'What's the trouble? You look a bit shaken.'

Karyn waited until they were in his study with the door closed before wondering how to broach the subject. If he knew exactly what was going on around him he might be prepared for any attempt upon his life. But if she said too much she might precipitate action. He seemed the kind of man who would do what he could to put matters right.

'Well?' he demanded, and there was a note of worry in his tones. 'Is it about Nerissa?'

'No, it's about you,' she replied, and having found the opening she needed, proceeded to tell him about Marfissa's visit. He listened with his face slowly turning pale, and she knew it was from anger and not fear. When she lapsed into silence he began pacing the room. Karyn watched him in silence, not wanting to interrupt his thoughts. Finally he halted and came to face her.

'This is a lot worse than I thought,' he said in low, urgent tones. 'I know they won't rest until I am removed. But I'm not afraid for myself, Karyn. It is Nerissa I'm worried about. She has suffered enough. I'm torn between two desires, and have been for some time. I want to break this stranglehold that Marfissa and his kind have upon the island, and I want to keep silent for Nerissa's sake. I shall be placing my life in jeopardy by helping the police, and if anything happens to me Nerissa will be pushed deeper into trouble. She would never recover. You saw Marfissa here last night!' His voice had an edge to it which she hadn't heard before. 'That proves just how much power he has over the islanders. What can I do, Karyn? Now that I've met you I feel even more reluctant to make the decision. I know which decision should be made. I know where my duty lies. My father was the same, and no doubt he would have forced a climax in this business if he had been spared. But now I am in his place and it is up to me.'

'You're a brave man, Paul,' Karyn said, wondering what she ought to do. If she encouraged him to help the police and he died as a result she would blame herself for the rest of her own life. With that knowledge in the front of her mind she could understand perfectly how he must be feeling. It would not be easy for any of them.

'Let us go out today, and I'll think it over. This evening will be soon enough to make the decision.' He sighed as he tried to relax, and although he felt easier in having decided something, Karyn knew the deadly moment of really casting his determination was still to come.

'I'll get Nerissa ready,' she said. 'We can leave when you like.'

'Perhaps you had better leave the island now,' he said, taking hold of her hands. 'I don't want to endanger your life, Karyn. Perhaps I ought to see Inspector Zoulas right now and take the vital step. No matter what happened to me, the island would be cleaned up and made fit for you, Karyn.'

'Paul, couldn't you leave here as Marfissa wants you to do?' she demanded. 'Nerissa is the only excuse you need. I don't want to exert any pressure on you, but you must not leave your decision too late. Do you think they want you to leave the island in the hope that once away from here they will have an easier job to get you?'

'Anything is possible, and I have many risks to run. Perhaps I have already left it too late. If Marfissa has decided that I'm too dangerous to be allowed to live then nothing will stop them attempting to kill me.'

'It's frightening,' Karyn said. 'This is such a beautiful island, and there's no indication of all the trouble lying under the surface of life here. Everyone seems so happy.'

'One day the appearances will match the facts,' he said gently. 'Karyn, I want you to know that I think you're the most beautiful girl in the world. Perhaps I'm beginning to feel melodramatic, but I wouldn't want to die without telling you how much of an impact you've made upon me. I know we're almost strangers, but sometimes two people don't need a long time to discover how important they are to one another. Do you know what I mean?'

'I think so, Paul.' She nodded slowly, and he took her into his arms. His mouth came against hers, and Karyn had never known such ecstasy.

A firm tapping at the door caused them to draw apart, and Paul went in answer. Karyn saw Miranda standing in the doorway, and the housekeeper's face was tense and showing fear.

'Loukas Benassis is here and asking to see you, Paul,' Miranda said. 'Did you send for him?'

'Benassis!' Paul shook his head, and Karyn saw none of the fear in his face that had shown when they had seen the old gypsy down at the harbour in Khalmia. 'I didn't send for him. What does he want, Miranda?'

'You know what he wants,' the woman replied. 'You will bring death into the house if you admit him. He wouldn't have come here without being asked. Have you finally decided to help the police?'

'Who is Benassis?' Karyn demanded, and her voice was stiff with dread. A sudden thought revolved in her mind and she caught her breath. 'He isn't the one who carries out Marfissa's orders, is he?'

'Marfissa's killer, do. you mean?' Paul demanded with a smile that barely stretched his lips. He shook his head. 'No. Benassis is a police agent. I don't know why he pretends to be otherwise, because everyone knows his real identity.'

'A policeman?' Karyn couldn't believe her ears. 'Then why were you afraid of being seen by him the other day, Paul?'

'Because Marfissa's men would think

I was telling him something if we were seen together,' Paul retorted. 'Zoulas knows that, and probably thought such an action would force my hand. Benassis has been dogging my footsteps for weeks. That's why Marfissa has been getting edgy. He fears that I'm on the brink of informing against him.'

'And now Benassis is here at the door,' Karyn breathed. 'What are you going to do, Paul?'

'Make that decision earlier than I anticipated, I suppose,' he replied, 'Miranda, will you ask Benassis to come in?'

'It is your life, Paul,' the woman declared.

'All I ask of you is that you do not contact Marfissa,' Paul said quietly.

'Miranda,' Karyn almost shouted. 'You wouldn't do that, would you?'

'Paul knows the situation better than you, Karyn,' came the swift reply. 'My husband comes first, and I have my orders the same as everyone else. Paul knows that, and he understands.'

'Tell Benassis to come in, Miranda,'

Paul said firmly.

'Shall I leave, Paul,' Karyn demanded as the housekeeper went off.

'Perhaps it would be better,' he replied. 'The less you know the easier it may be for you. Go and get Nerissa ready for travelling. When I've finished here we'll put her on the yacht and go away until Zoulas has done what he came to do.'

'But when you come back the situation will still be here, won't it?' she demanded. 'Marfissa's men will be waiting for their revenge, Paul. That's what Miranda told me.'

'Perhaps, but I'm hoping that when Marfissa is taken the islanders will realize that they are free at last and will make the most of it.'

Karyn could see that he had at last made his decision, and after trying to get something done she could not now attempt to change his mind. She sighed as she started from the room, but he caught at her and pulled her into his arms.

'Don't ever forget these few days that

we have known each other, Karyn,' he said, and kissed her quickly when they heard footsteps approaching the door.

'I'll never forget,' she promised, and opened the door and fled before the old gypsy entered the study to greet Paul.

Miranda was standing by the kitchen door, and Karyn hurried to the woman's side. The housekeeper was grave of face, yet showing tension and fear.

'What have you to do, Miranda?' Karyn demanded.

'I must telephone Marfissa and report this,' came the terse reply.

'But why? Isn't Paul entitled to your loyalty?'

'He is, but so is my husband, and something would surely happen to him if I fail to do what I have been told.'

'But that's the way Marfissa maintains his hold on everyone,' Karyn went on desperately. 'Can't you see that? Don't you realize that if you do nothing now the police will be able to make their arrests before Marfissa knows what is happening?'

'And by nightfall Michael will be lying dead in some lonely place.' Miranda shook her head. 'Paul did not try to stop me because he knows the penalty I would have to pay for not doing it. There is no other way, Karyn.'

Karyn sighed and shook her head, refusing to admit defeat. But there was enough fire in Miranda's dark eyes to warn her that she was wasting her time.

'At least wait a little while before doing anything,' she pleaded. 'Paul is taking us away in the yacht after Benassis goes. Let us get aboard before you telephone.'

'Make haste; I will delay as long as I dare.' Miranda turned away and entered the kitchen, closing the door behind her, and Karyn remained staring at it for long moments before she could recover her thoughts and hurry away to get Nerissa ready for their flight to safety . . .

11

None of this seemed real, Karyn told herself as she prepared Nerissa to travel. The girl said nothing, for Karyn had told her they were going out for the day. Shocks would come later, but Nerissa wouldn't be able to fight against the plan to leave the island because by the time she knew it would be too late for her to voice a protest.

'I'll carry you down to the *salotto*,' Karyn said, taking the girl into her arms.

'You're in a hurry,' Nerissa observed. 'Is the house on fire?'

'No. Paul asked me to hurry, that's all.' Karyn was breathless as they started down the stairs.

'Don't let him see that you're so eager to please. You'll spoil him, Karyn.'

'Loukas Benassis is with him in the study,' Karyn retorted, and the girl went very still in her arms. They were silent until they reached the ground floor, and then Nerissa spoke, going stiff with determination.

'Take me into the study, please, Karyn,' the girl commanded.

'But Paul is very busy.'

'I can tell that police agent more than Paul can,' Nerissa said firmly.

'You know he's a policeman?' Karyn shook her head in wonder. She didn't argue, but walked to the door, and Nerissa tapped and turned the handle quickly, thrusting the door wide. Karyn entered, staggering a little under the girl's weight, and Paul hurried forward to help her. Benassis stared at them, his face dark, and he looked picturesque in his gypsy garb.

'What are you telling him, Paul?' Nerissa demanded as they placed her upon a couch.

'This is not business for your ears, Nerissa,' he replied. 'You should not have brought her in here, Karyn.' His dark eyes were troubled as he looked at them.

'I ordered her to bring me here,' Nerissa said. 'I have to make a report if you are doing so.'

'What can you know about Marfissa?' Paul demanded.

'Only that he arranged for the accident.' Nerissa was tight lipped as she stared at her brother, whose face slowly lost its colour.

'The accident?' he questioned, his eyes narrowing. 'Your accident, Nerissa?'

'The one in which our parents died,' the girl said harshly. She looked at Benassis. 'Are you ready to hear what I have to say?'

'We have been waiting a long time to hear your evidence on this matter,' he replied gravely. 'If you will give me an outline I will be able to decide if Lanni Marfissa should be arrested. I can telephone Inspector Zoulas, who is waiting for the outcome of my visit here.'

Karyn listened while Nerissa repeated the account she had already been given by the girl, and this time Nerissa's voice did not falter. But there were changes in the evidence, and Karyn learned that Nerissa had been afraid to disobey Marfissa, although she feared that some method of killing her father had been prepared. Paul began to pace the study, his face closed, devoid of expression but showing harsh lines, and from time to time he paused to stare at his sister's intent face, and the sound of Nerissa's voice seemed endowed with the power to pierce their nerves and shrivel them. Karyn could not believe the half of what she heard, but Benassis seemed intent upon every word, and the old man's face indicated that he was certain he was learning the truth.

'So that was the way of it,' Paul said tensely when Nerissa fell silent. 'Father was killed because he stood up against the organization. I never even thought of it in that way. I believed the accident was truly by chance. No wonder you've been ill as you have, Nerissa, with all of this on your conscience! But you can rest easy now. The fault lies not with you but with me and others like me.

Even Father was to blame because he took so long to act. If only he had confided in me! Most of this trouble would have been avoided.' He turned to the policeman. 'Do you have enough evidence now to arrest Marfissa and those others with whom he consorts?'

'Enough to place him in custody, where he belongs, but the ordeal for you will not begin until his trial opens. However you can rest assured that when people learn of this evidence they will also want to talk. Inspector Zoulas has been impressing this point upon islanders for a long time, but no-one would ever believe him. But it is a simple truth, and will be made plain by the time Marfissa collects his dues from the law. May I use your telephone?'

Paul led the man to the door, and Karyn went to sit by Nerissa's side, her arm about the girl's shoulder. Nerissa looked pale, but her dark eyes held determination, and Karyn was relieved to see there were no signs of distress in Nerissa's face. Paul returned within a few minutes, and he was alone. He closed the door of of the study and stared at them, his face showing anxiety.

'I expect Marfissa knows of this already,' he said calmly. 'We have to get away from here as quickly as possible.'

'The yacht,' Nerissa said. 'Is it ready to sail?'

'I had it taken to the harbour at Khalmia yesterday because the sight of it upset you so, Nerissa,' he replied. 'But we can travel the back road to the town. Marfissa will probably use the coast road. He won't waste any time coming for me.'

'But the police,' Karyn said nervously. 'Won't they give you protection?'

'Undoubtedly. Benassis mentioned it. But the local policemen may very well be in Marfissa's bondage. They would not help us if the word was out against me.'

'This is dreadful,' Karyn said in unflustered tones. 'But we can't sit here while time is flitting by. What are we to do, Paul?'

'I think this does not concern you so

deeply that you have to risk your life by fleeing with us,' he responded gently.

'Nonsense,' Karyn returned strongly. 'Where you go I go. I refuse to stay behind. Nerissa needs me, and I can't bear to be parted from you.'

He smiled then, and opened the door again. 'I was hoping you would say that,' he responded. 'But we must hurry. Miranda was using the telephone when I showed Benassis to it. Marfissa knows now and the word will be out on us. I can expect no mercy, and they will not care who is with me if they catch up with me.'

He came across the room as he spoke and lifted Nerissa into his arms.

'No, Paul,' the girl said calmly. 'Put me down. I would be a burden on you. Take Karyn and get away from here. I deserve to stay behind for what I've done. If I hadn't been so scared by what happened I would have told you and the police sooner about the whole nightmare. But I was afraid of Marfissa. He used to come up to the attic to see me when you were not around. Miranda let him in. He threatened me all the time and I dared not go against his wishes.'

'He'll pay for all his wrongs,' Paul said, ignoring his sister's pleas, and Karyn followed him as he started from the room. They went out to the *piazza* and Paul hurried to his car. When he had placed Nerissa in the back he turned to Karyn, and took her into his arms. 'This is the girl I love, Nerissa,' he said, helping Karyn into the car. 'Don't forget that, Sister.'

Nerissa smiled happily, although her face was stiff with dread. Karyn tried to comfort the girl as Paul slid in behind the driving wheel, and relief flushed through her as the car pulled away with a jerk. They were running, but Karyn had a feeling that destiny had yet to play its hand. The enchantment that had captivated her from the first moment of her arrival here was throbbing inside her, and she could not feel fear or anxiety as Paul drove recklessly in a bid to get away before Marfissa could find them.

They didn't take the coast road. Paul turned inland, following a narrow, winding road that headed into the mountains. Dust arose behind them in the sunlight, and Karyn, glancing behind, realized that it would act as a beacon for any pursuer. But she couldn't really believe that Marfissa would attack Paul in daylight, with the police knowing that he might do it. Despite the incidents which had occurred, she could not accept that one man could control the whole island through fear and organization. A hundred years ago it might have been possible, but not in these enlightened days.

A sense of unreality began to grip her as she stared first at Paul's broad back as he sent the car along as fast as he dared on the treacherous road, and then Nerissa's pale face. The girl was slumped back in her corner of the seat, eyes closed, face grim and intent. Karyn could understand some of the emotion that must be crippling the girl. But she could not understand how Nerissa had bottled it all up inside her, forcing herself to be ill. But the girl had clearly been under the influence of Lanni Marfissa, the same as everyone else on the island.

They were thrown forward as Paul suddenly braked, and Karyn reached out to grab at Nerissa as the girl fell towards the front seat. She peered ahead anxiously and her blood seemed to run cold when she saw a car pulled across the road, blocking most of the way. Three men were standing before it, and she thought she saw sunlight glinting on weapons in their hands.

Paul had been travelling too fast to be able to stop short of them and turn the car around, and in any case the men would soon give chase, and they would take more chances than he dared with the girls in the back. He turned to glance at Karyn, and his face was set in harsh lines.

'Get down on the floor, both of you,' he said sharply.

Karyn did not argue. She looked ahead, saw the distance between them and the stationary car narrowing quickly, and realized that Paul was aiming for a space between the car and the edge of the road. She felt dizzy as she peered over the edge of the road and saw a steep drop of many feet. But she had no time to dwell upon the fear that came to her. She grasped Nerissa and pushed the girl down, trying to cover the girl as it gathered speed. She closed her eyes and pressed her face against Nerissa's shoulder.

Karyn thought she heard voices shouting, but the noise of the car filled her ears. She tried not to imagine the sheer drop at the side of the road as Paul steered towards it, and a slight bump told her when they were negotiating the most dangerous part. The car lurched violently and Karyn gritted her teeth as she thought they were going over the edge. The tyres protested shrilly, and then there were sounds like a car back-firing, and Karyn realized with a sense of unreality that they were being shot at.

She reached out and touched Nerissa's face, trying to reassure the girl. They were thrown to and fro as Paul struggled to retain control of the car. Then all sounds died away, and they were travelling fast along the empty road.

Karyn pushed herself up and looked around. They had passed around a bend and were clear, and for a moment Paul half turned to peer at her and she signalled that they were all right. She lifted Nerissa from the floor, and saw that the girl was animated by the danger. Nerissa was actually smiling as they settled back on the seat.

Karyn kept glancing back, and when she saw the car in pursuit, and gaining on them, she compressed her lips and took hold of Nerissa's hand. The girl looked back although Karyn tried to prevent her, and Nerissa shook her head and leaned forward to tap Paul's shoulder.

'They're gaining on us, Paul,' she said quickly. 'Drive faster.'

'They're more reckless than me,' Paul said. 'I'm afraid of putting us over the edge of the road. These bends are treacherous.'

'You know what will happen to us if they catch us,' Nerissa said.

'You're enjoying this, Nerissa,' Karyn accused, and the girl nodded quickly, her dark eyes alight with excitement.

'I'm not afraid,' she replied. 'But we shouldn't have brought you along. It is none of your business.'

'Keep your heads down in case they start shooting,' Paul commanded, and Karyn put an arm around Nerissa's shoulders and hugged the girl to her.

The road twisted and turned, climbing and falling through the hills, and Karyn tried to find some semblance of sanity in this affair. She was afraid, not for herself, but for Nerissa, and yet the girl seemed to be unafraid. There was more colour in the girl's cheeks than Karyn had ever seen.

Paul suddenly twisted the wheel and sent the car into a narrow side road, almost turning it over with the suddenness of his action, and Karyn felt her heart come up into her mouth as she was thrown against Nerissa. But the car remained on its wheels. Paul was staring behind, driving with one hand, only half his attention ahead, and Karyn looked behind and saw their pursuers go racing by on the other road. She sighed with relief as her tension lessened, and Paul, catching her eye, smiled and nodded.

'Sorry about all this,' he said quickly. 'But if we can get into town without their knowing we'll have a good chance of getting away from them. Inspector Zoulas won't waste any time acting upon our information, and with a little luck he'll grab Marfissa before any real harm is done.'

'Marfissa was in that car chasing us,' Nerissa said. 'I wish you had a gun, Paul. I would have used it against them.'

'Don't be so bloodthirsty!' he retorted, and returned his concentration to his driving.

Karyn kept watching the road at their backs. They were travelling along a rough track, throwing up clouds of dust with every lurch of the car, and once or twice Karyn saw stretches of the road they had left below them. She watched anxiously for signs of the other car, but saw nothing.

Paul was still driving as fast as he dared, not slowing for the bends and twists that taxed his driving skill to the limit. Karyn's heart was in her mouth most of the time, but she felt elated by the dangers, not scared. Once she stared across deep space where the hillside stretched away from them to shelve forward to the lower level of the coast, and she spotted the town of Khalmia in the distance. It was so near and yet so far away, and she wondered how many men Marfissa would bring in to get Paul.

They climbed a steep incline, and at the top there was a sharp bend which Paul saw almost too late. He braked and spun the steering wheel, trying to keep to the track. On the left was a steep slope down across some grassland, and it terminated in a sheer drop of more than a hundred feet. Karyn clutched at Nerissa as the car veered off the track and started plunging down the slope towards the precipice. Fear stabbed through her and she stared at Paul as he struggled to get control. The slope was getting steeper, and suddenly Paul threw a glance over his shoulder at them.

'I can't hold it,' he gasped. The brakes aren't working. Something happened on the bend. Can you jump out, Karyn? I'm trying to change down. Get out while you can.'

'Nerissa can't get out,' Karyn replied calmly, her eyes holding Paul's face for a moment before her gaze lifted to stare at the drop rushing towards them. 'We'll go over, Paul, unless you can steer to crash into that part of a wall over there.'

He nodded, his face grim, his eyes narrowed, and sweat beaded his forehead. Nerissa was clutching Karyn's hands tightly, as if her very life depended upon Karyn, but there was nothing Karyn could do to save her. It rested upon Paul's shoulders to do what he could.

Karyn was not conscious of panic or fear as they swept down the slope, leaping and lurching over the rough grassland. Karyn could see the sunny space beyond the drop, and far in the distance was the coast road. Nerissa was thrown against her, and then flung away again by the movement of the car, and Karyn stared at the girl as they lay in opposite corners. Nerissa's face was calm and composed, and Karyn realized that none of them had any fear. It all seemed so unreal. She couldn't believe it was happening.

The ruins of a stone wall clung to the very edge of the precipice, and Karyn took a deep breath as they bore down upon it. Nerissa was sitting behind Paul, and they were approaching the edge at an angle, with Nerissa seated nearest to the drop. The girl cried out once, just a sharp protest against what seemed inevitable, and then they were upon the wall, ramming it with such violence that large stones were flung out into space.

Karyn was hurled forward against the

back of the front seat. She reached out in an attempt to grab Nerissa, but missed the girl. The car crunched upon the old stonework, shuddering as it was brought to a violent standstill. Paul jerked forward, and Karyn winced when she saw his head strike the windscreen, which shattered. The next instant the front left wheel spun off the edge of the precipice and the car tilted sickeningly as if it intended slithering straight down into the valley below.

Nerissa screamed as she was flung sideways against the door, and Karyn reached out quickly, fighting her terror and shock, grasping the girl's arm and dragging her back. Paul slumped over the wheel, and the car settled down at an angle, the front wheel out in space. For tense moments Karyn sat as if turned to stone while loose bits of the wall went tumbling down through space. Dust filtered in the sunlight. Silence returned slowly, as if reluctant to cover the dreadful sounds of the impact.

'Paul!' Nerissa stirred slightly, and

the car shuddered and groaned as it slithered forward a fraction of an inch. The movement, though slight, started a miniature landslide of stones from the wall, and Karyn clutched at the girl, forcing her to remain still.

'Don't move, for Heaven's sake, Nerissa. Just sit still.'

'We'll go over the edge,' the girl said tensely, and they stared at one another, seeing panic mirrored in blue and brown eyes. Karyn held the girl's hand tightly. 'What shall we do?' Nerissa continued. 'If we move, the car will slide over the edge.'

'Just keep still,' Karyn repeated. 'Paul is unconscious. He struck his head. Can you see from there if he's bleeding?'

'No, I can't see. Karyn, what can we do?'

'The car is balanced here,' Karyn said, surprised that her tones were so matter-of-fact. 'Paul is almost out over the edge. If he could move this way a bit his weight will help to stabilise the car.'

'But he's unconscious, and if he moves as he comes round we shall go over. I'm frightened, Karyn. We're going to die.'

'Don't panic, Nerissa. Just stay still. I'll try and get hold of Paul. If I can drag him along the seat his weight will counteract against the balance.'

She leaned forward slowly, and there was a coldness in her stomach that was sickening. She could feel a tingling in her fingers and toes as she peered straight out at space, but she kept a strong grip on her nerves. The ruins of the old wall were holding the car back, and although the wall looked insecure because of the impact with the car, Karyn had hopes that it would hold. She stretched out her trembling hands and touched Paul's shoulders, but the movement caused the car to tilt a little, and her heart came into her mouth as Nerissa cried out in panic.

'Sit still, Nerissa,' she commanded. She did not change her position, and her fingers were touching Paul's back. She scarcely dared to breathe as she tried to get a grip upon Paul. When she leaned forward still more the car tilted again, and for one heart-stopping moment it seemed that nothing could prevent them from plunging down into the depths.

Karyn felt dizzy, and there was a buzzing in her ears, but she clung to her nerve and eased forward a little more. Grasping Paul's shoulder, she tugged gently but with all her strength, and he slumped back from the wheel and his head sagged sideways, towards her and away from the drop. The car moved again and Nerissa cried in anguish. Dust plumed up from the wall where the front of the car rested against it, and Karyn, staring fixedly at the spot, tried to will the stonework to remain in position. But she saw that the large stones were beginning to give way under the pressure, and she set her teeth and secured a fresh hold on Paul's shoulder.

Slowly she exerted her strength and braced herself to pull him along his seat. If he could be moved away from the drop there was a chance that the change in the centre of gravity would hold the car on the edge. It was their only chance, Karyn saw, and she prayed as she summoned up all her strength.

'You won't do it!' Nerissa cried. 'Can I help you? My arms are very strong from dragging myself around.'

'If you lean forward you may start the car on the move,' Karyn warned, 'but I can't do it alone. Paul is too heavy. Try it, Nerissa. Can you get forward on to the edge of the seat?'

The girl gritted her teeth and moved forward, starting the car rocking again. Karyn clutched at Nerissa and they stared into each other's eyes until the sickening motion had ceased. Then the girl moved again, and as she took hold of Paul's other shoulder she thrust out her feet to brace them against the back of the front seat.

'Now!' Karyn said through her teeth. 'Gently, Nerissa!'

They began to pull Paul along the seat, and each slight movement started the car rocking. It was like a see-saw, balanced there on the very edge of the drop, and Karyn could see a stream of small stones dropping away from the spot where the wall was supporting them. But they moved Paul, and the car seemed to settle back as his weight was moved from the left side. Karyn had the feeling that they would go sliding over the edge of the drop, but she fought the impulse to spring out of the car and get her feet on firm ground. She reached out and opened the door, throwing it wide, almost sending the car forward again with the movement, and she did the same with Paul's door, leaning far to the right in the hope that her weight would anchor them to the spot. Paul's door stayed open, and he sagged and slid half out of the car, his head and shoulders touching the ground. He was still unconscious.

'Nerissa, drag yourself across me and get out of here,' Karyn ordered. 'Be quick!'

'I can't move,' the girl said. 'My legs.'

'You moved your legs just now, when

you took hold of Paul,' Karyn said quickly. 'You moved under stress, Nerissa. I didn't realize it at the time, but you moved your legs.'

Karyn stared down at her legs, her face twisted with emotion. 'I can feel pain in them,' she cried. 'They've come alive.'

'Move now, and hurry,' Karyn said. 'Get up slowly and move by me. When you get out take hold of Paul and hold him. You can drag him out of the car if it starts slipping again.'

'And you?' Nerissa said.

'After you,' Karyn retorted.

The girl took hold of the seat with one hand and grasped Karyn's shoulder with the other. Karyn watched her closely as Nerissa stood up, supporting herself with her arms. Then the girl lifted one leg and set her foot past Karyn. She followed up the movement by sliding her body across Karyn, and then she took another step and got out of the car.

Karyn closed her eyes as the car lurched sickeningly. She heard Nerissa scream, and opened her eyes to see the girl grasping at Paul's shoulders. It was time to get out! She forced strength into her own limbs and levered herself up, throwing herself out of the car as quickly as she could. She sprawled on the ground beside Nerissa and clawed at Paul's shoulders with the girl as the car heeled up in the air. For a moment it seemed that Paul was caught fast in the car, but their combined efforts overcame the obstacle of his weight and he came tumbling clear, falling upon them and knocking them in a heap. They clung to his limp body as the car disappeared with a protesting screech of crumpling metal as its weight bore it against the wall, which disintegrated and spilled outwards into space, followed instantly by the car. A few moments later there was a terrific crash far below, and Karyn closed her eyes and uttered a prayer of thankfulness.

When she opened her eyes again Nerissa was getting uncertainly to her feet, and Karyn reached out a hand and caught at the girl's hand.

'Be careful. Your legs may not support you at first. Don't be impatient, Nerissa.'

'I can walk,' the girl said dazedly. 'It must have been the shock, but I can feel life in my legs.' She stared at Karyn with disbelief in her dark eyes, and then burst into tears.

Karyn bent over Paul, and saw with relief that he was slowly regaining his senses. As he opened his dark eyes and peered dazedly at her Nerissa uttered a shriek of fear. Looking up, Karyn saw the girl gazing at the road above then, and she stared in the same direction, catching her breath when she saw the car that had been pursuing them coming into the hidden bend much too fast.

Paul sat up, clutching at Karyn as he saw how close they were to the precipice. Then he spotted the car, and his arms went around Karyn's shoulders as the sound of screeching tyres reached their ears. They watched spellbound by shock, and saw the car leave the track and come plunging straight down the slope as they had done. Marfissa was at the wheel, and Paul cried out as the man tried to swing the car around. Karyn saw the front wheels turn. The car slid half around before the steepness of the slope betrayed it, and Nerissa screamed as the vehicle toppled over on to its side.

With horror in their faces they watched the car roll over and over towards the precipice, and there was no wall to act as a barrier for it. The car shot off the edge and into space, where it described an arc through the sunlight as it fell swiftly below, carrying its passengers to their deaths. The sound of the impact came clearly to their ears, and a second later Karyn saw a burst of flame engulf the stricken vehicle. She turned away and closed her eyes.

'Let's get out of here,' Paul said softly. 'Lanni Marfissa won't care about us any more.'

He got to his feet and helped Karyn up, and she saw surprise flood his face when Nerissa stood up shakily and took her first tentative step up the slope. Then he laughed, and the sound dispelled most of Karyn's shock. He pulled her into his arms and kissed her soundly.

'There was something about you that first day you walked into my study,' he said softly. 'I had a feeling that you would be able to perform miracles. It hasn't taken you long to prove me right. I love you, Karyn. Don't ever leave us, will you?'

'Never,' she said shakily. 'At least, I'll stay as long as I'm needed.'

'Then you'll never go,' he said happily, and kissed her again. His strong arms held her close, and his expression told Karyn many things. They started up the slope together, and there was pure joy in his voice as he called to his sister. 'Hey, wait for us, Nerissa.'

Karyn watched the girl as she climbed the slope. Nerissa was revelling in her returning strength. The girl was unsteady on her legs, but she was walking, and that was all that mattered. Now destiny looked like living up to its promise, and if she doubted it at all then the strength in Paul's arms about her earned their own proof.

We do hope that you have enjoyed reading this large print book.

Did you know that all of our titles are available for purchase?

We publish a wide range of high quality large print books including:
Romances, Mysteries, Classics
General Fiction
Non Fiction and Westerns

Special interest titles available in large print are:
The Little Oxford Dictionary
Music Book, Song Book
Hymn Book, Service Book

Also available from us courtesy of Oxford University Press:
Young Readers' Dictionary
(large print edition)
Young Readers' Thesaurus
(large print edition)

For further information or a free brochure, please contact us at:
Ulverscroft Large Print Books Ltd.,
The Green, Bradgate Road, Anstey,
Leicester, LE7 7FU, England.
Tel: (00 44) **0116 236 4325**
Fax: (00 44) **0116 234 0205**

Other titles in the
Linford Romance Library:

FAR FROM HOME

Jean Robinson

At 23, Dani has an exciting chance at a new life when her mother Francine invites her to live with her in Paris and join her fashion business. What's more, Dani has fallen in love with Claude, Francine's right-hand man. But it's anything but plain sailing at home in England, where Dani has been living with her father, who is on the edge of a breakdown from stress and doesn't want her to leave. What will Dani choose to do — and is Claude willing to wait while she decides?

LEAVING LISA

Angela Britnell

At age seventeen, married with a three-month-old baby and suffering from post-natal depression, all Rosie could see was her life in a cage with a giant lock. Twenty-five years later, after having left her husband Jack and daughter Lisa, she runs her own business in Nashville. But while she's in England, she sees an engagement announcement in the newspaper — Lisa is getting married. And Rosie decides she wants to make contact after all these years, despite fearing their reaction. Will they find room in their hearts for her again?

RUNNING FROM DANGER

Sarah Purdue

Pregnant and alone, Rebecca flees to the US in a bid to escape her ex and his ties to organised crime. There she meets Sheriff Will Hayes in a small backwater town — but can she trust him? When she tries to make a run for it, Will stops her and suggests a plan that involves them both. But Rebecca is unsure of his feelings for her. Can Will keep her safe from her ex and his crime-boss father? Or will the biggest risk come from falling in love?

COOKING UP A STORM

Judy Jarvie

Artist and entrepreneur Amy Chambers runs a quirky but popular café and art studio in Derbyshire with her sister Lorna. When they win the chance to be mentored by a celebrated business angel who will assist with their expansion, it's an exciting prospect — until Amy realises it will put her head to head with the country's most renowned celebrity chef and global gourmet, Mal Donaldson, who takes no prisoners. Can Mal find a way to convince her that together they have the perfect ingredients for lasting happiness?

THE EIGHTH CHILD

Margaret Mounsdon

Why is Posy Palmer the only one to be concerned when her old school friend, Iris Laxton, disappears? But as Posy begins to delve into Iris's past, she realises how little she really knew about her. When Posy's bicycle tyre is deliberately punctured, and evidence begins to disappear, the only person she can turn to for help is Sam Barrington, the charismatic ex-policeman who accused her of wasting police time when she reported another missing person six months previously. Will he believe her this time?